What You Don't Know About Men

What You Don't Know About Men

Short Stories

by

Michael Burke

iUniverse, Inc.
Bloomington

Several stories in "What You Don't Know About Men" originally appeared, sometimes in slightly altered form, in the following publications: "Eulogy," in *TriQuarterly* and *Tartts Three*; "Patsy" and "Things That Matter," in *American Way*; "The Boys" and "Punch Drunks," in *Sport Literate*; "Keepers," in *Private Arts*; "No More," in *The Prairie Light Review*; "Alamo," in *Third Wednesday*; and "Big Love," "Eddie Doyle Says Life's Been Good" and "The Jonquils," in three Polyphony Press anthologies, *The Thing About Love Is…*, *The Thing About Second Chances Is…*, and *The Thing About Hope is….*

iUniverse books may be ordered through booksellers or by contacting:

iUniverse
1663 Liberty Drive
Bloomington, IN 47403
www.iuniverse.com
1-800-Authors (1-800-288-4677)

ISBN: 978-1-4620-2279-3 (sc)
ISBN: 978-1-4620-2280-9 (e)

Printed in the United States of America

iUniverse rev. date: 5/13/2011

Book design and cover photograph: Sheila Sachs
Author photograph: Michael Caplan
Editor: Ilene Slonoff

This book is dedicated to
ROBERT CHARLES

and to the memory of
MYRTLE M. BURKE,

with love and thanks.

non sum qualis eram

"Your fathers, where are they? And the prophets, do they live forever?"
Zechariah 1:5

What You Don't Know About Men

TABLE OF CONTENTS

Eulogy

I know what they will say
when I am dead.
They will say, "Matthew Connors
should have tried harder."

Kent and I are driving along the flat, two-lane roads that reach across northern Illinois, the narrow, black-topped highways that stretch among the cornfields of Midwest, middle-class, middle-of-the-road America. Kent is my younger brother. He is seventeen years old. I am driving.

Kent got high with friends last night and was left at a party on a farm in Hinckley. Maybe you know how to find Hinckley. I needed a map. "I think it's near Rockford, maybe," was all Kent could say when he finally telephoned this morning.

Kent says nothing now and just sits close to the door, with the sun and wind on his face. He wears a black T-shirt, black pants and black boots. He also wears a tiny silver earring.

Kent turns off the radio when I turn it on.

"I almost forgot to tell you," he says. "Tommy Burns is dead."

I manage to keep my eyes on the road.

Kent tells me that Tommy Burns, who was my brother's age, was found three days ago hanging in his bedroom closet. Kent tells me that Tommy was naked and that a pants belt looped around his throat had been fastened to a wooden ceiling beam. Tommy, Kent says, had been jerking off. The idea of the belt was to cut off oxygen to his brain until the very moment he came, thereby doubling-tripling the impact of his orgasm.

Kent smiles when he tells me the next part: Tommy was found by his older brother.

"Jesus," I say. "Jesus" is all I can think of to say, until I think to add, "Whatever happened to plain, old-fashioned fucking?"

When we get home, Kent drops himself onto the couch and I head upstairs to Carol's bedroom. Carol is my sister. She is fifteen years old and blonde, the only blonde in the family.

Her bedroom door is closed and I know better but I enter without knocking. Some guy is lying on her bed. He's younger than me, but taller than me, and I ask him his name.

"Todd," he says. He's only wearing bicycling shorts. The bed sheets are kicked down around his feet. He uncrosses his legs. "Who are you?"

The way he asks the question makes me suddenly think that, if I had to, I might not be able to take Todd in a fight. I haven't been in a fistfight in years and Todd looks like he lifts weights.

"Where's Carol?" I say.

"In the bathroom," he says. "Who are you?"

I walk down the hall to find the bathroom door closed and locked. I hear water running. "Carol?" There is no answer. "Carol? Kent's home. He's okay. He's sleeping downstairs." There is still no answer. "Carol?"

Todd shouts from the bedroom. "I know," he shouts. He's still stretched out in bed. "You must be Carol's brother."

I have no doubt that our parents love us.

My father is a happy man who cherishes his wife and adores his three children. He owns this, our big home in the suburbs, and he laughs when I ask if his job downtown is important. He has been a vice president at a Loop bank for as long as I can remember.

My father is an alcoholic, too, something he came close to admitting once—and only once—on an icy February night, when both our eyes were filled with belly-laugh tears after we'd spent the past forty minutes struggling to walk on drunken legs from the garage to the back door of our house.

He grabbed my arm, squeezed tightly, gained his balance. His eyes were all of a sudden focused and filled with fear.

"You must hate your old man," he said.

Two nights later, when Dad was drunk again and I sat right down at the kitchen table to join him with a can of beer, my mother stepped in from the dining room and crossed her arms. She looked at us with mean, frustrated eyes.

My father laughed his sick drunk's laugh and said, "Damn. Some men have wives who love them."

My mother uncrossed her arms. "Don't say I don't love you," she said, "because you might make it come true."

I had witnessed this fight before, many times before, and usually I just stayed quiet, waited it out, until Mom returned to her bedroom so Dad and I could resume drinking. But on that night, Mom stayed and stared and I did the unthinkable: I raised my can of beer toward her.

"Relax," I said. "Have a drink."

She stepped forward and cracked the grin off my face with the back of her hand. "I am trying to save your father's life," she said.

This all happened when I was eighteen years old and Dad and I were such good friends. Now, I am nineteen and my mother is still trying to save my father's life. From that night—the night my father saw, through blurry eyes, his wife slap his son—he sincerely tried giving up booze. He went a few weeks without a drink and then he drank again. Then he went a few months without a drink and when he started to waver, my mother came up with the idea that they, just the two of them, should take a long driving vacation out west. My father embraced the idea and within a week they were gone, leaving me to look after Kent and Carol.

So I have no doubt that our parents love us. But I have come to learn that there are priorities in love. And at this moment in our love, my father is the first priority.

> *I know what they will say*
> *when I am dead.*
> *They will say, "Matthew Connors*
> *should have known better."*

We live in an old Chicago suburb with brick homes, narrow streets and tall trees. The night sky is dark, but to the east—taller than the tops of the village square shops, but lower than the lowest clouds—is a bright, orange neon cross. The cross is fixed to the steeple of the Catholic Church, but on some nights it looks like an electric angel.

When I was five-and-a-half years old, in fact, my best friend Andrew convinced me the electric angel had come down from heaven, hunting for me. The story goes that I ran away in fear and wasn't found by my mother until close to midnight, but I don't recall running away. I do remember Andrew's lie.

Andrew is still my best friend and he still lies. He lies about the cash he owes me and swears he's "definitely paying back tomorrow." He lies about the car his stepfather is supposedly buying him, "a black Porsche," while he still every day drives his sister's old Camaro. He lies about girls, too, including his sister.

Jody is a year older than Andrew, a year older than me. She wears a lot of makeup. Andrew always told me that Jody hated me, but one night at a party, Jody corners me outside the bathroom and says, "Let me tell you something, something you'll want to hear." Indeed, it is something I want to hear, am surprised to hear, am even somewhat frightened to hear: Jody wants to fuck me and she wants her friend Marie to fuck me, too, because they have never fucked the same guy before and they want to compare notes.

"What do you say?" she says.

"Well," I say.

"Andrew says you've always wanted to fuck me," she says. "Do you know Marie?"

"Sure," I say.

"'Sure' you know Marie, or 'sure' you'll do it?"

"Sure I know Marie," I say. "And, sure, I'll do it, sure. Yeah."

"I'll call you, soon," Jody says and disappears for the rest of the party. Three days later she telephones before 8 a.m.

"Tonight," she says. "Your house."

At one point that night Jody bites my lower lip and it bleeds.

Later, when I'm still on top of Marie—dark, expressionless Marie—Marie sighs and tells me, "I balled your little brother once."

In the early morning, a few hours after Jody and Marie have left arm-in-arm, I walk upstairs and run into a Korean kid I knew from high school. Kim is only wearing underwear. He looks like he has either just woken up or hasn't gone to sleep. He's laughing, loudly, and I think he's still drunk or high.

He doesn't seem at all surprised to see me and he playfully punches my shoulder. "'Blondes have more fun,'" he squeals, stumbles into Carol's bedroom and closes the door.

I walk down the hall to the bathroom, where the door is closed and locked. I hear water running. "Carol?" I say. There is no answer. "Carol? Are you okay?"

Mother telephones long-distance every other day to tell us where she is, where they're going. She left us an itinerary of their stops, but she uses these telephone calls to more or less check in and to let us know that they're on schedule.

She talks like a postcard: "Drove through the Painted Desert. Saw the Grand Canyon. We'll be done with Yosemite by noon tomorrow if you need to reach us. Your Dad is doing just fine."

When I don't say anything, she asks, "How are things?"

For a moment, I consider telling the truth. Your youngest son is a drug addict. I haven't talked with Carol in weeks. Last night at a party I ran into this girl Marie, who I fucked in your bed three days ago, and Marie didn't even recognize me. She walked up to me and said, "Hi. My name is Marie. Are you from around here?"

Instead, I tell my mother that everything's fine. "Everything's fine," I say. "Can I speak with Dad?"

I hear her hand the phone over to Dad and I know I've made her mad: She knows she and I can't seem to talk, but Dad and I can talk about nothing for hours. "Hello, son," my Dad says and launches into a detailed description of the Petrified Forest. "Hell," he finally says, "this call must be costing a bundle. How you doing, anyway?"

I almost tell him the truth, too. "Come home," I almost say, but instead I say, "I'm fine. We're all fine. You two be careful out there." And we laugh.

My father always taught me to count on the family, but I have come to realize that you can only really count on yourself.

"I'll talk to you later, son," he says now.

"Good-bye."

"Good-bye, son," he says and hangs up.

You can only really count on yourself. From beginning to end, you're on your own.

I know what they will say
when I am dead.
They will say, "Matthew Connors
should have been stronger."

Andrew calls to ask if I have seen or spoken to Marie. She's missing and Jody is worried. I tell him I haven't seen Marie since the last party. Andrew says that maybe the electric angel got her, and we laugh. Andrew asks if he can come over so we can get high. He says my little brother sold him some pills.

"That's my little brother," I say. "What are you waiting for?"

That night, late, Andrew and I are eating pizza and watching MTV in the dark. The phone rings and rings and it takes me forever to answer.

"—Let me speak to Andy," a girl is saying.

"Jody?"

"Let me speak to Andy," Jody says. "They found Marie. Marie is dead."

"What?"

"She killed herself. With pills. Where's Andy?"

"Jesus," I say. I tell Andrew to come to the phone. "Marie killed herself," I tell him.

"Yeah," Andrew says. He's moving slow. "It's been a tough week for everybody."

At the wake for Marie two nights later, I try standing in the back of the funeral parlor, as far away from her body as possible. A man I have never seen before steps in front of me and stuffs a pair of gray, flimsy gloves into my hands. "You'll use these when you carry the coffin," he says. He's a thin man leaning over me and when I look surprised—this is the first I've heard anything about serving as a pall-bearer—the man squints and says, "Well, you were her boyfriend, weren't you?"

When I don't respond, he squints more and leans closer. "You were her boyfriend, weren't you?" he says again.

"Yes," I say. "I guess . . ."

When the man turns away, Andrew slips through the quiet crowd and tugs on the gloves. "What are these?" he says.

"The guy thinks I was her boyfriend or something."

Andrew kind of shakes his head and kind of smiles. He slaps two pills into my palm. "Take these," he says. "You look like shit."

When I hesitate, my best friend Andrew tells me, "Take them," and I do. Andrew grins. "Everything's fine," he says.

Everything's fine, I tell myself, and then a woman yells, "No."

She is a dark, short, heavy woman dressed in black and I think maybe she is Marie's mother. She is standing near the sofa at the front of the room and she yells "No" again when I realize that she is pointing toward the coffin, where her daughter lies and where my brother alone is standing.

Kent is wearing one of my old sports jackets that is even too small for him. He leans forward and kisses Marie's lips.

"No," the woman yells again and Kent leans forward and kisses Marie once more. Then two guys who look like cousins grab Kent from behind and pull him away from Marie and toward the parlor door. Kent is crying. The cousins are swearing and when I try grabbing Kent, one cousin shoves me away. They take Kent out onto the sidewalk and as I step outside they push Kent and punch Kent and Kent falls to the ground. They swear some more as I try to help Kent stand. They watch as I wrap my arms around Kent and drag him toward my car. He's out cold and I have a hell of a time putting him into the passenger seat.

When we get home, he's still out cold, but I don't think he's out cold from the fight or from grief. I think Kent has just seen too much in too few years. I drag him inside and carry him upstairs to his room. As I undress him, I remember that I cannot remember the last time I put my little brother to bed.

I walk down the hallway to the bathroom door, which is closed and locked. I hear water running. "Carol?" I say. "Carol, open the door. We've got to talk." There is no answer. "God damn it, Carol, open this fucking door," I say and after a moment, I haul off and kick the door, breaking it open, slamming it open against the inside wall.

I nearly scream.

Carol is standing facing the mirror in the harsh white light of the bathroom. She has shaved her head.

She slowly, calmly, turns to face me and her reflection turns, too. All I see are the bald twin heads of someone, something, that used to be my sister.

"Yes?" Carol says and raises an eyebrow. She puts a hand on her hip. "What shall we talk about?"

I know what they will say
when I am dead.
They will say, "Matthew Connors had it
coming. What was his problem anyway?"

Kent has been asleep for hours. Carol is in her room, at last. Just before midnight, Jody shows up, says she wants to spend the night with me.

"I know what you mean," I say and we go to bed.

In bed, Jody rolls me onto my back and kneels across my waist. She murmurs something. Without saying a word, I hand her a gray, flimsy glove from the wake. She puts it on. I put on the other.

In the dark, I close my eyes. I feel Jody's gloved hand brush my cheek, then grip my throat. With my gloved hand, I touch her shoulder, then grasp her neck. She murmurs something again and bends forward so I feel her breath in my ear.

"I hate you," Jody whispers.

I feel weight all over me. I find I'm choking for breath. My eyes are stinging. "Yes," I say. "Yes."

Big Love

Tom leans back and plows his long fingers through his thick, wet-with-sweat hair. He closes his eyes and here, in the darkness of his bedroom, he whispers. "Patrick," he says, "tell me that you love me."

I catch myself groaning, then, close my eyes, too. I'm on my back and Tom is kneeling across my thighs. "Come on, Kincaid" he says. "Tell me that you love me."

Tom and I: We've been through this before. I sigh, open my eyes. "I love you," I say, and Tom sighs, too, lifts his chin, then, shakes his head. He lowers his face and looks down on me.

"Just once," he says, "I'd like to hear that from someone who's *not* handcuffed to my bed."

"Yeah," I say, squirming just a bit. "Well," I say. "You better get these off. I've got to pee."

Tom starts scrounging on the nightstand for the key. He can barely see without his glasses. As he's leaning over me, I lift my head and kiss his flat stomach, which makes him giggle.

"That tickles," he says.

"Yeah," I say. "Well, you better hurry."

In the bathroom, with the door closed, standing in the bright light before the mirror above the white sink, I think about Tom and love and how I kissed his stomach, how I hoped that kiss would make him feel better, how I did, in fact, love Tom—cared for him, felt for him—but how my love was different from the love he desired, than the loved he asked for, than the love he wanted to hear.

When I return to the bedroom, Tom is curled beneath the sheet, on his side, facing the closed window. I slip into bed behind him, pull our bodies together and kiss the back of his warm neck. He murmurs something.

Tom turned thirty-one last week, so I pull close enough to whisper in his ear.

"Tommy," I say. "Good night." I know that calling him Tommy makes him feel younger.

Tom lives with a lawyer named Victor. I have never liked Victor, which is maybe why I still sleep with Tom every now and again. Why Tom sleeps with me is his business. I suppose it has to do with love.

My current boyfriend—and I use the term for lack of a better phrase—is named Wheaty. When I met Wheaty—at a New Year's party hosted by twin lesbian painters in Bucktown—I asked if everyone called him Wheaty because his pony-tailed hair was the color of wheat. He raised his thin eyebrows and just looked at me for nearly a minute.

"No," he finally said. "Everyone calls me Wheaty because my name is Wheaty."

"Oh," I said.

"It's short for Wheaton," he explained.

"Oh," I said again. "Well, how do you like the artwork?"

Wheaty and I slept together that night and we've been sleeping together, more than less often, since. I was walking through Lakeview after work yesterday—yesterday was really the first breezy, spring day we've had this year—when it occurred to me that I hadn't slept with anyone besides Wheaty in quite some time. That realization might have been another reason why I called Tom.

Wheaty is six years younger than me and he's still living the part of his life in which he calls every man he meets, "Jim." . . . A dark-haired man at a hotel bar: The guy will light Wheaty's cigarette and Wheaty will smile his thin smile and say, "Thanks for the smoke, Jim." . . . A stocky redhead getting off the Red Line subway: Wheaty will brush shoulders with the guy, smile, lower his eyes. "Oh," he'll say. "Pardon me, Jim." . . . A new waiter at one of his favorite coffeehouses: Wheaty will actually wink, then smile, then say, "Hey, Jim, what's new?"

I once yelled at Wheaty to stop all of this flirting, but he merely shrugged and said, "It gives me a sort of Lauren Bacall air." Then he narrowed his eyes before I could say anything else. "A *young* Lauren Bacall," he added.

Tom is dressed and in the kitchen now. I'm still in bed, but Tom's closet is open and his gray suit jacket is hanging on a hanger off the doorknob. Tom is a lawyer, too.

I hear him running water for the tea kettle and opening the refrigerator door, probably grabbing a bagel, which he always eats plain. I kick the sheet to my feet, sit up in bed and stare again at the suit coat. I start wondering how much time I've spent with Tom, how many nights and mornings we've done this same thing.

"You're awake," he says.

He's standing in the bedroom doorway now, dressed except for his jacket, swallowing a bite of bagel. His eyes are bright behind round glasses.

"You look sleep-deprived," he says. "How much did we drink last night? You want some bagel?"

Before I can say a word, the telephone rings. It must be seven o'clock. Whenever Victor is out of town—this time it's New Orleans—Victor always calls Tom at seven o'clock.

"Let me get that," Tom says, smiles and disappears.

Before I met Wheaty, before I met Tom, I lived for five months with a realtor named Frank. I suppose I thought I loved Frank. He was a few years older than me and he owned a condo. I was shocked, devastated, when he eventually told me that he had fallen for some new guy, some new guy who owned a condo, too.

Two weeks after Frank dropped me, I was on my brother's roof, helping him nail new shingles to his old suburban home.

"We better take a break," I remember Sean saying. "This is hot work."

We set down our hammers, crawled our way up the peak, and started passing a plastic bottle of water back-and-forth between us.

"Kathy," my brother said—Kathy is Sean's wife; I tell her just about everything—"Kathy," he said, "tells me you just broke up with that guy."

Sean had seldom referred to Frank or any of my gay friends. Calling Frank "that guy" would've normally set off my temper, triggered a fight; but, on that afternoon, Frank was pretty much just "that guy" in my thoughts, as well.

"Yeah," I said. I sipped some water and passed the bottle back. Sean and I kept from looking at one another.

"Well," my brother finally said. "That's gotta be tough. You okay?"

"I'm fine," I lied.

From the corner of my eye, I could see Sean nod and gulp a big swallow of water. He wiped his mouth with the back of his hand, then, passed the bottle back to me. Wiping his mouth like that, sitting this close: Sean reminded me so much of Dad.

"You sure?" Sean said and our eyes connected only briefly.

"Yeah," I said. "I'm fine. Really." I swallowed some more water, then, turned my face to see Sean clearly. "It's just that Frank—that asshole—still has some of my power tools and disco records."

My brother nodded, his narrow face full of genuine understanding. And then he couldn't help but laugh.

When he didn't stop laughing, I said, "What's so funny?"

"Nothing," Sean said, shaking and grinning and still laughing.

"What?"

Sean looked at me hesitantly. "'Power tools and disco records?'" he said. "That's just something you'd *never* hear a straight guy say."

After a moment, I started laughing, too. But I shoved Sean's shoulder, anyway, and told him to go fuck himself.

Tom returns to the bedroom, still smiling. He walks passed me to the closet, slips into his close-fitting jacket.

"You better get up," he says. "I've got to get to work." Then he leans toward me and kisses my mouth.

"How's good ol' Victor?" I ask, then, wince.

"I better brush my teeth," Tom says.

After Frank, I met Tom and we started having sex. Tom—Mr. Corporate Lawyer by day, Baron von Pleasure by night—introduced me to a variety of harmless party toys: blindfolds, handcuffs, a rainbow of flavored rubbers, which are an acquired taste, to be sure. But a little kink was exactly what I needed to forget Frank.

Tom and I both somehow knew we'd never really be more than friends, nothing other than buddies who fooled around from time to time as we stumbled through life looking for Big Love. "Big Love" is Tom's phrase, I suppose because "Mr. Right" sounds a little silly.

At a Boystown bar one night, I asked Tom if what he had with Victor was Big Love and Tom shook his head, looked at the crowded dance floor, said, "No, no, no."

Then he spoke louder to hear himself above the music. "But it's the closest I've ever come," he said. "Maybe the closest I'll ever get—and that's what scares the hell out of me."

A few weeks before Frank dropped me, my father suffered his first stroke. My brother's wife Kathy had called that morning with the news. "You better get down to St. Agnes fast," she had said. "Sean's getting dressed."

I was living on the city's north side and St. Agnes Hospital was on the south side, but I arrived about fifty minutes before Sean and Kathy. The old man was laid up in a regular room and looked better than I expected.

"Where's your brother?" he said.

"On his way," I said.

"Good," Dad said, closing his big eyes.

"How you doing?"

When Dad didn't reply, I asked again. "How you doing?" When Dad didn't reply the second time I knew better than to ask a third. His sullen silence had little to do with his stroke.

We sat in the white quiet of that little room until Sean and Kathy arrived. Sean rushed toward Dad's bed, grinning hopefully, saying, "Hey, old man. Nothing but cakes and ale?"

"Nothing but cakes and ale," our father replied.

At the same time, Kathy walked over and hugged me. "How are you doing?" she asked.

This all happened three years after Mom had died. From a stroke. Same hospital.

"Me?" I said, only then realizing the tears welling in my eyes. "I'm fine," I said. "I'm fine."

"Patrick," Tom says. He's standing in the bedroom doorway with his arms crossed. "Come on. Get dressed. I've got to go. I'm late."

I groan and get out of bed. I'm feeling stiff when I stretch and when Tom tells me to hurry again I say, "I'm hurrying, honey, I'm hurrying." I smile, hoping I sounded like Victor. I bend to pick up my underwear from beneath the handcuffs on the floor.

"I'm getting too old for this," I mumble.

I toss the handcuffs to Tom and he proceeds to watch as I get dressed. Tom has always gotten a kick from watching me dress and undress, and, now, he just stands there, not smiling, not blinking, just watching.

After I zip up my jeans, I sit on the edge of the bed to lace my boots. Tom looks toward the bare, hardwood floor between us.

"You and Wheaty," he finally says. "Big Love?"

I can't help but smile at the notion. But I gently shake my head, whisper, "No."

Tom nods, gives me a swift glance and frowns. "Well, Kincaid," he says, "maybe someday." He clears his throat, tosses the cuffs onto a pillow and turns. "Let's go," he says. "It's late."

Dad had been worse than he looked, which shouldn't have come as a surprise. That was Dad all over. The next morning I visited him in the hospital again. Of course, we didn't say much and we looked at one another even less.

But just as I was preparing to leave, my father spoke. "Before you go," he said. His voice was much weaker. His eyes were wet.

When he didn't continue I stepped back to his bed. He raised his big hand to cover mine resting on the thin railing.

"Before you go," my father said, "tell me that you love me."

This time I was well aware of my tears.

"I love you," I said. "Dad, I've always loved you."

He nodded, then sighed, then closed his eyes. "Yes, son. Good night, son. And thanks."

My father didn't say another word. He died that night.

I make it through another day, thinking that maybe there is no perfect love, thinking that maybe it's "coming close" that counts. Love is really a small, fragile thing, I think, and yes, that seems unsatisfactory.

"Unsatisfactory" was a word Frank had used often.

When I get to Wheaty's loft for supper, we know better than to ask each other too many questions.

"How was work?"

"Fine. How was your day?"

"Just dandy."

Neither of us inquiries about or even mentions the previous night.

Later, in bed, in the darkness once again, the two of us naked between warm sheets, I get an idea. I try to blindfold Wheaty with an old necktie, but he objects.

"How come?" I ask. "Doesn't it turn you on?"

Wheaty gives me one of his raised-eyebrow looks again.

"I've been blindfolded before," he snorts. "It's the color I detest. I mean look at it. It's peach."

I groan and ask Wheaty what difference the color could possibly make.

"Peach? Believe me," he says. "Peach matters. If there's one thing I know, it's how to accessorize."

I laugh softly and kiss his cheek and press our legs together and pull myself close beside him. Wheaty: He smells like fresh sheets.

I turn my face into the pillow. I whisper his name. I whisper, "Tell me that you love me."

"What?"

I have to wait a long time before I can get around to repeating myself. My eyes are closed. I think I am pretending that I am not really there.

"Tell me that you love me," I say again.

"Oh, Jim," Wheaty says. He's whispering, too. He wrestles onto his side so he can put his arms around me. "Are things that bad?"

Happy Hours

The idea, like all of his good ideas lately, came while he was drinking.

A book, Dick Sullivan thought. A coffee table book with heavy, white paper and rich, textured photographs of the best hotel bars in America. The Round Robin at the Willard in Washington, D.C. The Bookstore Bar at the Alexis in Seattle. The lobby of the Algonquin in New York. The lobby of the Palmer House in Chicago and the lobby of the Pfister back home. *Yes.* And, woven throughout: a winding, wistful essay—his words—examining the decisive role hotel bars have played in the unfolding American drama.

"You want another?" The bartender, a fellow Dick Sullivan's age with roughly the same stocky shape and retreating hairline, was shaking the ice at the bottom of a Collins glass.

Dick Sullivan smiled widely and replied eagerly. "Certainly," he said.

The bartender did not smile. He grabbed the glass and turned.

Dick Sullivan was spending his first of two weekday nights at the Lincoln Hotel in Springfield, Illinois. A teen-age girl with wet, stringy hair was scooping a basket of popcorn out of a brightly lit, noisy machine next to a blinking, out-of-order jukebox at the other end of the cramped bar. To her left, near three tall windows, a skinny, tattooed man and an even skinnier, tattooed woman dressed in black shorts and T-shirts spoke quietly, earnestly, at one of three small, round tables. Behind shabby, bluish curtains and smudged glass, and beyond the boarded-up shops in the two-story buildings across the street, the State Capitol dome rose in a tarnished, autumn splash of evening sunshine.

"Oh, why not?" Dick Sullivan added aloud, still smiling. He called to the bartender. "Let's make it a double!"

The bartender grunted but did not turn.

Dick could see the man's sagging face reflected in the wide, chrome-framed mirror mounted behind the bar. The bartender wore a black shirt with a stiffened collar and black trousers that were hemmed just a bit too short.

After a moment, Dick Sullivan nodded, now convinced his book could be a Great Book—a tale of Big Men and Big Deals, an epic yarn of dreams created and dreams crushed in America's clubbiest watering holes. *Yes!* He might even convince Mary to shoot the book's photographs.

Mary Kelly was Dick's drinking buddy back home in Milwaukee. She lived upstairs and across the hall in their old apartment building and with her frizzy, silver hair she was the person who most fascinated Dick Sullivan.

Mary was a lapsed Catholic, staunchly pro-choice, adamantly opposed to the Vatican's prohibition of women from the priesthood, and an outspoken critic of what she called the Pope's "tyrannical powers." Yet, she pined for the majesty of the Latin Mass and conceded that she now and then missed the comfort of a dark confessional.

"But I have to tell you," Mary once explained over bottled beers and a pasta-and-sausage supper in Dick's sparse apartment. "Listening to Nina Simone is better than going to any church."

Mary was an artist: a painter, weaver and black-and-white photographer whose taste in music ranged from Vivaldi to Coleman Hawkins. Her one-bedroom apartment was cluttered with unfinished projects, sprawling plants and an incense named Tranquility, which always lingered into the hall but only rarely crept down the narrow, darkened stairs to Dick's door. She shared her apartment with four cats she named the Marx Brothers. "The one who never meows? That's Harpo."

For money, Mary Kelly taught painting, drawing and pottery to wizened senior citizens at three different rehabilitation centers across town. She would frequently arrive home cursing, "Those old Krauts are going to be the death of me. We'll just see who buries whom!"

The bartender planted a fresh highball in front of Dick Sullivan. "Four thirty-five," the bartender muttered, rubbed his flabby neck, and walked away.

As Dick scrounged for his wallet in the breast pocket of his sports jacket, he imagined traveling across America with Mary, bouncing from hotel bar to hotel bar, taking graceful portraits and scribbling furious pages of penetrating observations. *Hotel bars are more romantic than taverns,* he thought, *and boasted more flavor than a thousand saloons.* Dick Sullivan swooned with the notion of happy days and happy nights, enjoying margaritas and mai tais with Mary as they kicked back after long days of hard artistic labor.

Dick wondered just how many words a guy would actually have to write to fill a book. *Not that many,* he surmised.

He placed a crisp five dollar bill on the bar top, smiled warmly upon Honest Abe and gingerly gripped his wet glass. "Here's to fooling some of the people some of the time," Dick toasted aloud to no one and took a big swallow.

For nearly the entirety of his adult life, Dick Sullivan had sold insurance to businesses (mid-sized manufacturers, mostly, as opposed to corporate giants or mom-and-pop shops). His work had taken him from one coast to the other and though he had almost always stayed in two-star hotels not unlike the Lincoln, he often cocktailed in the better establishments. Among his co-workers, Dick Sullivan was renowned (and, behind his back, ridiculed) for his love of life on the road.

"I've never been to San Francisco," Mary had told him one late morning. The two were lounging in her cozy sun porch, which overlooked a narrow back yard. They were reading the Sunday *Journal-Sentinel* and nursing a tall pair of Bloody Marys.

"You," he replied, smiling over the top of the sports pages. "You would love Frisco."

"I've never been," she repeated. After a moment, she added, "In fact, I've never been west of the Mississippi. Been to New York. Lived in the Keys with my first husband. But never been west."

Their conversations often snaked back to their previous marriages: two apiece, all four ending in divorce. The failure of Dick's second marriage and the Oh-This-Again complications of another divorce ultimately rattled his own belief in Catholicism. He began thinking of organized religion as little more than a commercial transaction, not so different from the insurance policies he sold to protect against calamities everyone prayed would never occur.

"You and I, Dick," Mary said on another occasion, a stormy, spring evening as she carefully refilled their heavy glasses of Merlot, "we're not made to settle down, I'll tell you that."

Actually, Dick Sullivan had always thought it was the women he chose for wives who weren't made to settle down. Both were redheads and always on the go: work, coffee with this friend, shopping with another, volunteering at St. Pat's or visiting neighbors. Dick had never told Mary that both of his marriages ended because his wives had become entangled in affairs. Instead, he simply nodded, lifted his glass, and toasted, "Here's to never settling down!"

The truth is, Dick Sullivan thought, *I would be happy to settle down.* As much as he enjoyed the business travel (for years, being on the road enabled him to dodge the emotional earthquakes that rocked his life back home), he could feel himself slowing, aging, wanting to rest.

"May I take the popcorn out to the pool?" The teen-age girl, grinning widely, was juggling three heaping baskets of popcorn in her thin, freckled arms. The bartender grunted and the girl replied, "Thank you."

She reminded Dick of his own daughter. Something about the teen-age girl's surprising politeness carried an echo of Bridget's manner. Bridget was grown now, living in Janesville with another woman and a baby of their own. Bridget was the child of his first marriage and Dick Sullivan realized he seldom spoke of her to Mary. In fact, he had managed to never mention Bridget's girlfriend, though he had acknowledged the baby. In part, Dick Sullivan justified his silence by rarely mentioning his son, as well. Brendan was from his second marriage and had moved last year to attend college in New Orleans. Dick wondered if Bridget and Brendan ever spoke. *Probably not. Probably won't—until I remarry . . . or die.*

Dick cringed and chuckled uncomfortably with that last thought before gulping more bourbon.

Mary Kelly had never had children. "Oh, I could have had kids, and don't think both husbands didn't want them," she explained dryly. "But my paintings, my photographs, my art—they're the only children I ever desired."

Mary could get away with saying things like that to Dick. Neither Dick's first nor second wife would have said anything remotely similar; if they had, Dick Sullivan was certain he would have guffawed. He only laughed at Mary Kelly when she herself was laughing or when they were together, enjoying a grand time such as the hot, summer, Saturday night they spent listening to Puccini and mixing "surprise" drinks for one another. The drinks were derived from recipes—Brown Foxes, Palmers, Horse's Necks and so on—in one of the few, old, yellowing books in Dick's apartment.

"I'm just so angry at you!"

The woman's shriek startled Dick Sullivan and he spilled his drink onto the bar top. He looked over his shoulder to see the skinny, tattooed couple fighting.

"Quiet down now," snapped the man.

"Why can't you face the truth?"

"Me?" The pitch of the man's voice rose sharply. "The truth? What about you?"

With that, the woman chucked the remnants of her icy drink into the man's face, bolted from the table and dashed out of the bar into the lobby of the Lincoln Hotel. The skinny man shouted after her, stood and froze.

He swiped his face with both hands. He glanced at Dick Sullivan, who automatically smiled without thinking.

The skinny man sputtered, "What makes you so happy?"

Dick blinked.

"Well?" the man demanded. "What have you got to say?"

Dick did not know what to say. His smile flattened.

Finally, the skinny man swore and stomped stiffly out of the bar.

"Well," Dick murmured, dabbing his dampened hand with a small, white napkin and twisting back in his seat on the barstool.

The bartender was rinsing glasses and, despite the commotion, had not turned.

Dick raised his voice to attract the bartender's attention. "Then here's to love," Dick said, lifted his glass and swallowed the last of his drink. The bartender still did not turn.

Yes. Well, Dick thought before speaking loudly toward the bartender's reflection: "So here's to yet another great American success story!"

The bartender straightened his back and sighed deeply. He wiped his hands on a rumpled bar towel and turned to face Dick. "What is it? You want another?"

Dick Sullivan smiled widely.

"Certainly," he replied. "Why not? And why not make this one a double, too?"

As the bartender grabbed the glass and turned away, Dick Sullivan looked out the window. Twilight shrouded the white and gold Capitol dome. He pictured Mary Kelly shuffling home, grousing about her doddering clients, lighting another stick of Tranquility. He imagined spending the night with Mary, their first, somewhere on the road. And he pictured himself telling her everything. *Everything.* He remembered Bridget from years ago, as a proper little girl, saying, "Thank you." Always in plaid and always so proper. He remembered trying to calm Brendan, always a rambunctious boy. "Be still, Brendan. Be still." And for a moment Dick Sullivan considered telephoning Bridget in Janesville and calling Brendan in New Orleans, too—talking to the daughter and son he had not spoken to since—*now, how long has it been?*

When the bartender placed a fresh highball on the bar top, Dick Sullivan tried smiling again and asked in a softer, smaller voice, "Hey, friend. Can I ask you a question? Did you ever think of writing a book?"

The bartender made a face. "Look," the guy said, shrugging. "I'm just a bartender."

And Dick Sullivan felt his throat go dry. "Yes," Dick Sullivan mumbled, looking down. He was no longer smiling. "And I sell insurance."

Alamo

A dark-haired woman with red lips is fiddling with my belt buckle and even if she wasn't speaking Mexican I'd be too drunk to understand. I just bend my neck back, pull a small, fringed pillow from behind my head and cover my face. I feel the woman tugging at the front of my jeans and to me (despite her rolling words, despite the musty smell of the dusty pillow, despite the ringing headache I've got from this piss-sour tequila) to me it sounds like she's saying, "So, talk to me, kid."

I was born in the heartland, I tell her. Malta, Illinois. My older brother, Fran, was run over by a freight train when he was fifteen years old. My sister, Ronnie, got pregnant when she was sixteen. She left town with the baby's father, who was twenty-seven. They might have hopped the Soo Line to get away; no one knows for sure.

Both my parents drink, which I didn't even notice until I met a Christian family new to town and the father of that family (his name was Mr. Hill) asked if my father or mother ever consumed too much alcohol.

"Well, yeah," I replied and Mr. Hill's thin eyebrows arched high above the gleaming golden rims of his eye glasses.

"Give some thought to your possibilities, son," Mr. Hill told me on another occasion. "Do you trust what I say to you?"

He had invited me to sit close beside him on his paisley sofa. "Life happens fast," he said, placing a nervous hand on my right knee. "Can you keep a secret?" He squeezed my knee firmly. "Life's almost over before you even know it."

I never told Mr. Hill that my parents fought a lot, too, which didn't bother me much, but scared the hell out of Mercy, our fox terrier. My father would shout, my mother would yell and the dog would scamper down the hallway rug, nose open my bedroom door, spring onto the mattress and rouse me with his sniffing.

Me? I am seventeen years old and I really miss Mercy.

I hear my best friend, Chris, groaning in the next room. We're in some back-road dive outside San Antonio; these little rooms have beaded curtains, no doors. Chris grew up in Malta, too, and to me (despite the exaggerated moans of our two sagging whores, despite the bouncy squawks of our two wooden cots) to me it sounds like Chris is saying, "Tell her how we got here, man. Tell her."

There's really not much to tell, I say. I could stand Dad punching at me, but the night Mom took a swipe, I snuck outside beneath Chris' bedroom window and stood on barefooted tiptoes to hear him whisper, "Man, we gotta get out of this town."

We left right there and then. Chris had been living with his big Uncle Red, who was himself no picnic. Uncle Red worked at Del Monte with my father and liked to warn us, "Steer clear of that candy-assed Hill."

Chris and I did what Ronnie did and what Fran had probably been trying to do: We hopped a freight train. A few weeks later—after passing some long, sticky nights in St. Louis, after spending a crazy spell teasing some buggy old guy with nine fingers in Kentucky—Chris and I finally ended up down here in Texas.

Along the way, we've had to scrape together some money, so we've done what we've had to do: everything from panhandling on Louisville street corners to smashing backdoor windows with alley bricks. Chris has always done all of the talking whenever there's been any talking that had to be done. I always got the better grades, but Chris is tall, straight-standing and one year older. He's the natural born leader.

I remember another August morning back in Malta, not too many hours after Chris had spent the sweaty night driving Tammy Boyd around the cornfields in his Uncle Red's pickup. Tammy Boyd was a chubby friend of my sister. She smoked.

"Tammy," Chris said, then pressed two of his fingers beneath my nose and laughed. "You should call her."

Tammy Boyd and I went that very night to the old, falling-down barn on the back of Mr. Hill's property. Afterward, Tammy started crying.

"We better put our clothes back on," she said and I asked about her tears.

"I was just thinking about your sister, Ronnie," she replied, hitching up her jeans. "How happy she must be, wherever she is. Do you think Chris loves me?"

Love wasn't something folks in Malta talked about much and love certainly wasn't on Chris' mind earlier this morning. Hanging around the Riverwalk here in San Antonio, Chris met a skinny, freckled kid, a year or two older than him, named Rudy. The two of them (with their shirts off and tied around their waists, sharing a bottle of Rudy's warm tequila) started yammering to me about how much money we could make if we started having sex with the businessmen who came to town. Chris and I are supposed to meet Rudy tomorrow morning, at the Alamo, to discuss the possibilities.

I feel the whore shaking my shoulders and when I open my eyes (I must have passed out) I can't tell if any sex has happened, but it's clearly time to transact business. The whore is standing beside my cot, swinging the pillow with one hand while holding her other hand flat as the farm fields behind Mr. Hill's old house. I remember that day on the couch and how Mr. Hill looked at his hand on my knee and started weeping.

"Five dollars," the whore tells me, in plain English, without a hint of emotion.

"Well, hell," I say, scrounging in my pants pocket for the five Rudy had given me. "An advance," Rudy had explained. Then he informed us about this place.

When I hand the whore the five, she smiles. I smile back because I think it's safe. Then, she points to a small bruise on my right thigh.

"Oh, yeah," I say, starting to squirm, not quite understanding.

The whore says something in Mexican and points to a small bruise on her left arm. She moves her blackened bruise up close to my eyes, to make sure I see it, I guess. Then this woman says something else, folds her hands together, shuts her eyes and starts praying. I watch her red lips moving with each mumbled word and I find myself all of a sudden wanting to please her, so I close my eyes and begin praying, too. But I don't really know any prayers, so I do the best I can.

"Thank you, Lord, for the gifts we are about to receive," I hear myself saying. "Amen."

The Kiss

Papa comes home, strides through the back screen door, grins—*Hello, hello, hello, I'm home.*

His beige work shirt is spotted with grease, much of it hard black still and looking shiny fresh. Papa's been working down south. Haven't seen him since summer started.

Mother shakes her red head, wags a chubby, pointing finger, then sweeps across the kitchen toward him with arms opened wide—*Look at you, look at you, you're a mess but I love you large.*

And they hug and they laugh, deep, from-their-bellies-and-throats laughs, chestnut eyes fixed into chestnut eyes and Papa kisses Mother, on the mouth, and they laugh again.

Papa glances over Mother's shoulder, then, looking at me—*How are you, Billy? How's school? How's*

But Dee-Dee comes running, squeezing past me on tippytoes through the dining room door, shoving me with little girl hands as she squeals—*Daddy, Daddy*—she squeals—*Daddy Daddy Daddy you're home!*

—*I'm home, D-girl, I'm home*—and Dee-Dee jumps and Papa bends and their arms are around one another, her little chest pressing against his big chest.

—*The grease!*—Mother shouts—*Your clothes: Watch the grease!*

And Dee-Dee's head is pressed against Papa's warm smooth sticky neck and Papa is sighing ooohhing aaahhhing, then arching his eyebrows toward Mother as if to exclaim—*Sorry, honey, sorry about the grease!*

But the dog starts barking and barking and barking, scampering at

Papa's big feet, sniffing and pawing Papa's wet work boots, wanting to jump—*Hey, boy! Hey, Ranger! Hey old boy, old Ranger!*

And Papa squats with Dee-Dee still stuck on him and Ranger jumps high enough now to lick both their faces and that makes Dee-Dee scream—*Yah! Yuck! Papa Ranger Mom!*—and Dee-Dee turns to Mother—*Mom? Mommy?*—*Yes, honey, here, honey, another mess*—and Mother lifts Dee-Dee in her arms, wiping her cheeks with the counter dish towel.

—*Yes, Ranger boy, yes, I'm home*—Papa, still squatting, now rubbing the dog's big ears, kissing then kissing then kissing the dog's mouth and nose.

—*Hey*—I say—*Hey.*

—*Old Ranger boy, good Ranger boy*—

—*Hey, Papa*—

And my father looks at me then, chestnuts twinkling, and he rises and I feel his shadow in this sun-brightened room. He pats the dog's head and steps toward me, one step, then, another until he's moved across the small room and around the low table to stand before me.

—*Hello, Son.*

And I feel myself leaning forward, inching upward on bare feet, eyelids shutting and I am swooning.

—*Son*—my father is saying—*William? Hello, Son.*

And when I open my eyes, Papa's hand, his big hand, his stiff reddened calloused hand is forward toward me. He's even shaking it, to get my attention and he says—*Son*—and I say nothing and the two of us shake hands, my growing hand lost in his sticky hand, shaking squeezing holding touching moving up then down, then up again, and Papa smiles.

—*It's good to see you, Son. You're growing up so fast.*

—*Get washed*—Mother shouts—*get washed, get cleaned, change clothes, let's eat, you're home, come on, excuse me, Son.*

And Mother and Papa rush around me toward the bathroom and Dee-Dee chases after them and Ranger scampers after them, too, barking and barking and I look down at my thin hand, smudged slightly with my father's work grease and I remember other evenings, Septembers past, when Papa would come home and kiss Mother's red face and squeeze Dee-Dee's little body and rub the dog's ears and stride toward me and smile and look down on me as I closed my eyes and kiss the top, the very top, of my head and I'd feel his kiss on my scalp, wet and warm and big in those days, and I remember myself squirming then, saying—*Papa*—saying—*Papa*—saying—*kissing's just for girls.*

Keepers

There's waking up and there's waking up. Listen, man, I know what I'm talking about. I know what I'm saying, man, this isn't just some horseshit, bullshit, mind-fucking talk-talk spewing from some big-chested, honey-potted mannequin quoting Scripture, shouting orders or even reciting dead-beat poetry, man. This is the *gen*, the nut, the straight, the truth. This is what happened, man. The fuck-you story of my fuck-you life.

Semper fi.

I wake up on the Belmont rocks—I don't wake up in the early-early morning, man, but later, I don't know, nine or ten; late enough, I guess, but not really late for me, not really, honestly, if you come to think about it, not really late for any of us, really. So I wake up, man, hot—it's July, blue-sky July, and it's so hot that the sky is shiny, the lake is shiny, the rocks are shiny, even the dry insides of my eyes are shiny, man—I'm hot, sticky, hot on the inside, too. So I wake up, man . . . slowly . . . *yes*, I always move this slowly, *yes*, I'm too young to be this stiff, *yes*, I know this kind of life is no kind of life for me, man, but fuck that and fuck you: IT'S MY LIFE.

So I wake up, man, hot and slow, and the first thing I think about is the first thing these days I always—*always*—I mean always always always always think about: Stuart. Where's Stuart? How's Stuart? Why's Stuart?

Stuart.

And that's when it hits me, man. That's when I realize, that's when I see. That's when it dawns on me. That's when I "Get The Picture, Son." That's when bells ring. Whistles blow. Birds sing. Rivers flow.

I'm just a bug, man.

Not a toe-steppin', heel-stompin', cane-crushin', squash-me-up-in-a-Kleenex, hold-me-at-arm's-length, rush-me-toward-the-open-second-story-window bug.

N-O.

I'm a fat ass, big-as-life, tie-me-to-your-bumper bug—tie me to your fucking bumper, man, then cut off my head and stuff my empty skull with feathers and paste, then mount me proudly on a wooden plaque above your gray stone fireplace and hoist your glasses in a toast to me on New Year's Fucking Eve, man.

"Bagged this one on Belmont," you might say, with your chin protruding. "Amazing specimen. Last of its breed."

Last of its breed you better hope, motherfucker—or Stuart, sweet Stuart, dear Stuart, *my* Stuart will be fast over here with a hacksaw and some rope, ready to trophy you.

Wasted.

Wasted.

Wast-ed.

Wast-dead, I think.

I've got to be out of my mind, what's left of my mind, what shattered pieces you could scrape together from the shrapnel of my mind, at least. This is one bad ass nightmare, I think. This is one fuckin'tripforthebooks, I think. Crazy time. Kray-zee. Sleep it off, shake it off, "Keep A Grip On Things, Son."

Semper fi.

I wake moments minutes hours days weeks years decades fucking generations later and nothing's changed.

"Well fuck this," I think and try to move. But I'm on my buggy back with my little buggy pincers pinching at the sky—and I don't think I'm moving, though I hear the shell of my back scrape against the concrete of these flat rocks.

"Well fuck me," I say aloud and when I hear my voice, I'd squirm if I could squirm, I'd flinch if I could flinch, I'd scream and kick and holler if I could do any of those, but all I can do, man, is cringe—cringe the way I used to cringe all the time—as a kid . . . and over there—a from-my-belly, inside-out, God, please, get-me-the-fuck-outta-here cringe.

Semper fucking fi.

The old man leans forward.

"If I am going to tell you anything about Mother," he says, "I suppose I should start with the scar—a tiny, pale scar now, still there after all these years, just where her right eyelid meets the pencil-thin, chocolate brown eyebrow she still until this morning drew on with the practiced patience that has always accompanied her particular brand of vanity, which I have come to call 'forgivable vanity,' the sort of vanity that comes from too many nights of dreams and too many days without money."

The old man narrows his eyes. He is sitting at a kitchen table in an Evanston townhouse. He already has explained how he never quite got used to the fact that he and his own mother were so close in age.

"My mother's scar is a scar that has looked back at me," the old man says, "whenever I have lingered a glance upon her face. A scar that I have seen above eyes opened wide—wide with the lake blueness of adolescent joy, wide with the red rage of drunken anger, wide with the white frozen smiles found in family photographs."

The old man sighs. He has not had much sleep, but he has asked you to let him talk.

"I have even seen this scar above big eyes filled with the big tears of shame," the old man says. "And now, today, this night, standing there in the warm, dim light beside my mother's hospital bed, I saw this tiniest of scars still there, silent, above eyes closed now forever."

Stuart.

"Roy," Stuart says to me. He's standing on the rock ledge above me, leaning, looking, big-eyed, red-eyed, scared. "Roy," he says again, "is that you?"

Is that you, I think. Is this me? Am me, me? Am me, I? Am—God, please, get-me-the-fuck-outta-here—

"Yes," I say and Stuart gasps.

He slips, falls, lands on his slender ass. He's still gasping and I suppose he sees my pincers pinching at nothing but air, excitedly, uncontrollably. I suppose he sees my shell glistening in its hardness. The thought scares even me.

Stuart shouts for Jody and Buck, Jody and Buck, Jody and Buck. He yells "help" "you guys" "help" "come here." He starts crying, too—and all the time, man, all the time, stares at me with those big beautiful bountiful boss eyes.

A bug's eyes, I think . . . and my heart sinks.

Jody and Buck, Jody and Buck, Jody and Buck, he calls, and those two finally run up close.

"Man," Buck says to me, "we've been looking all over for you. I figured we'd find you here."

Buck has short hair and eyes the blue they use to color Christ's eyes in all of those paintings. Buck attempts one of his standard-issue, all-purpose smiles, but I catch him cringing—an inside-cringe—but I catch it just the same. Buck has never served, but he's almost—*almost*—as sick as I am, so I know he knows the cringe.

Stuart has gotten back on his feet and now they're all three standing, looking down on me. Stuart's eyes are wet. Jody's mouth dips open. Jody is tall and toothy and he scoops the stringy hair out of his skinny face. Jody is young and from New Orleans. He's looking at me, but he's saying: "Oh Stuart, oh Stuart, oh Stuart." He says: "Oh Stuart, oh Stuart, oh Stuart . . . Is *that* your boyfriend?"

Oh, Stuart, I think. Oh, yeah, tell me all about it. Tell me something I don't know.

"Look at those . . ." Jody says, still gawking at me, but pausing now to search for a more tender word. He's wagging his finger at my face and arms. ". . . sores," he says. "And what's that smell?"

Stuart raises his hand to cover his mouth and nose. "It's Roy," he says, looking at me with big beautiful bountiful buggy bugged-out eyes now filled with one thousand tears. "It's him," he says. "It's him."

La vida es corta, y la muerte larga.

My mind drifts, my thoughts skip, my imagination rises toward the clouds. I see Lincoln Park filling up by now with people, people just like you: taut, tight-assed, big-lipped women jogging on your tippytoes, tits bouncing, a happy-sappy golden retriever leashed to your wrist . . . happy-sappy rich boys with sun-browned thighs and backwards baseball caps speeding past on your mountain bikes . . . one S.U.V. after another S.U.V. pulling into the parking lot, slipping into spot after spot after spot.

The park is coming alive with people just like you—but, man, I'm not worried about . . . "discovery." I'm down on the rocks and even though Stuart and Jody and Buck are standing on the ledge above me—bracing against the sight-smell of me—I'm not worried, man, because the people like you who come to this park aren't the sort of people who see us when we stand, who hear us when we scream, who give more than a passing thought to our tears.

The park is coming alive but I'm just about dead-as-a-doornail and Buck's just about dead-as-a-doornail and Jody and Stuart are this close to being dead-as-doornails, too . . . in your eyes. So I'm not worried, man, about . . . "discovery". . . because even Christo-Fucking Columbus couldn't discover us.

Jody looks at me, says: "Look at it move. What're we gonna do with it?"

Stuart is palming his face, shaking his head. Buck is, for the moment, silent. I know I know what Buck is thinking.

Buck is thinking, "This is it, this is the future, this is *my* future—and holy shit."

Jody widens his eyes. "Push it in the water?" Jody thinks he's come up with some bright idea—give the boy a lollipop, high-five me, man—but this lanky oyster cracker doesn't worry me, either—nothing, man, no thing, no body, no one, *nada nada nada* has worried my sorry ass for a long, sorry time.

But a thought does cross my mind: Stuart, oh, Stuart.

"I'll get a stick," Jody says and turns, but Buck grabs the back of his shirt, says, "No."

Buck, I knew I could count on.

"That's Roy, man," Buck explains to Jody. Buck gives Jody one of his patented, all-time-favorite trust-me smiles. "Roy is not an 'it,'" he explains slowly. "Roy is Roy. Can't you tell? Can't you see? Don't you understand?"

Buck and Jody are a couple, yes, they're an item, yes, they're *pal-zee wal-zee*, see? Buck, of course, is a thousand times sharper than Jody, but Jody's got a nice thick hammer, Buck says, so Buck lets Jody hang around.

Right now Jody is squinting at me and I know he's having trouble believing. He shakes his shaggy head. Poor kid. I have trouble believing, too.

Buck squeezes Jody's shoulder, then squats closer to me. "Hang on," he whispers in my ear. "We'll get you home. We'll get you home."

Home, I think. *Wow*, I think. Kiss my ass, plant a tree for Israel, weeee-doggie! Home.

Shit.

Home.

Sure.

Home.

Sure.

Home.

Sure . . .

Buck knows better but he nonetheless smiles warmly. I guess I should've known I could count on Buck for this.

After you've been sick—or after you've been in battle, anytime you've been this close to death, spent this much time in nose-to-nose, wait-til-He-blinks talk-talk with the Grimmest of Reapers—you learn lickety-split who you can count on. And let me tell you something, man: There's not many people in this Silly Putty World you can trust. Go ahead, take a head count. Sound off. Mark 'em on the big board. Johnny, tell them what they've won!

I'll tell you who I can trust: Buck. Buck and Mrs. Baines.

Buck, I met here, in Chicago, before I got sick. Buck isn't his real name, but who needs a real name in a world like this? Buck is from one of those Sheridan Road families up north, the sort of money-falling-out-of-their-pockets families where they don't put slipcovers on the couch because they never sit on the G.D. couch anyway.

Buck I met at a sidewalk cafe on Halsted when he asked to bum a cigarette off me and I was down to my last smoke.

"I'm down to my last smoke," I explained, but Buck gave me one of his like-I-give-a-fuck smiles. Sweet.

"I *need* a cigarette," he said. "Give me one." And I did.

There's never been anything—"anything," Jesus, listen to that word—there's never been anything between Buck and me, which is a whole other story. Let's just say that Buck is happy with Jody—and he's been happy with all the long line of Jodys who've come and gone before this current, for-the-time-being Jody.

Buck reminds me a lot of Mrs. Baines, the only other person I could count on. Mrs. Baines was from Maple Park, my hometown. She was an old bag even back when I lived there and she used to work in the bean fields, sweating a dirt-sweat for ten hours and a few dollars a day. Mrs. Baines used to come home at night and sit her wide ass across her rickety porch after supper and when I ran passed her house she always—*always*—used to lean forward and yell: "Stop running! Stop running! You have NO idea where you're going!"

Mrs. Baines was right. True-bluer words were never spoken.

I had no idea—no no *no* idea—where I was going and after Mrs. B fell face down in a bean field one dark and warm afternoon, she retired . . . and eventually stopped sitting across her porch . . . and eventually stopped yelling at me . . . and eventually faded away . . . the Big Adios.

. . . Me? I enlisted in the fucking Marines, man, and was shipped to Lebanon, that's L-E-B-A-fucking N-O-N Lebanon, man.

"Keep A Tight Shot Group, Son."

"yes, sir."

"Keep Your Head Down, Son."

"yes, sir."

"Nice Ass, Son. Mind If I Put My Hand Here?"
"why no, sir. not at all."

Semper fi.

Let me ask: Who do YOU trust?

I can't trust Jody. Sure, he's easy to look at it and he means well. But the world, man, is up to here with well-meaning cuties—and, let's face it—Jody, man, isn't sick, but he's more wiggy-wigged than I am—and, look at me: in your eyes, man, I'm a fucking beetle bug.

Here's something else I should say: I don't trust Stuart, either. I know I know I know. I say I love him—and I say I don't trust him. Well, listen, man, I've never understood why so many people so often confuse love with trust.

I love Stuart. I do. I do. Yes, I do. But that doesn't mean I automatically, no-questions-asked, yes-I-realize-I'm-waiving-my-right-to-counsel trust him . . . and if you've got a problem with that, so be it: It's Your Problem, Good Luck, I Wish You All The Best, Bon Voyage, Happy Days, Eyes Forward Son, fuck you if you don't understand me.

Amen.

I met Stuart two nights ago—what now, man? You don't believe in Love At First Sight?

Stuart came to my apartment to deliver some groceries from the agency. Stuart was born in Quincy—let's hear it for us small-town boys!—and he's new to town and new to the agency, too. He volunteers at the agency because it's like going to confession: It makes him feel all good about himself. *Mea culpa.*

"You've got beautiful eyes," I said to Stuart as he held my apartment door to leave. His ruddy face was lit by moonlight.

"So do you," he said and then I blushed—my first blush in about one hundred years—and I knew then it was love.

I can still blush, I remember thinking. *There's still hope . . .*

Capital L-O-V-fucking E. Love!

After all, what is love but hope?

Amen, brother, Amen.

The old man sits back, lets his long face lean sideways into the autumn sunshine that's just sneaking through the kitchen curtains.

"I am a man who likes to remember," he says. "And when I think about Mother's scar, I cannot help but recollect the old days, our early days, back when my little brother, Frank, was still in diapers. Our Maple Park days—the long, twilight summers playing hide-and-seek through the hot, dusty cornfields. The porch-step suppers, where we balanced paper plates on our knees and Mother bribed me to finish my canned peas by offering the promise of fresh-cut watermelon.

"I remember, too," the old man says, his jaw growing tighter, "Red's pickup truck grinding across our gravel driveway after Mother had kissed my sticky forehead, pulled the bed sheet to my waist and paused before closing my bedroom door to whisper tenderly, 'Sweet dreams, baby.'

"Red—with his curly beard and heavy work boots—would come, every night it seemed, like a too-warm summer breeze blowing long and low across the county plains.

"'Hullo, baby,' he'd always growl to my mother as our front screen door slapped shut behind him.

"And, then, I'd hear the muffled giggles—Mother's—and, then, the snap-fizzles of a pair of beer cans being opened simultaneously.

"'Mom, I need a water,' I said one night, my eyes misted with the weak sleep of a quiet child, but stinging from the sudden harshness of the bright overhead light in the kitchen.

"'Baby,' my mother exclaimed in a voice more surprised than angered.

"She was standing on her tiptoes, her back pressed to the kitchen sink, her arms stretched out as far as they would go around Big Red."

The old man pauses, takes a breath and nods his head full of memories. He bites his lower lip.

"Mother was naked from the waist up," the old man recalls. "And Red was naked from the waist down. I cringed.

"'*Kee-rhist*,' Red shouted. 'How come he's awake?'

"'Baby,' my mother said again, this time almost pleading as she rushed toward me, bending forward with her skinny elbows cocked against her stomach to hide her breasts.

"'I need a water,' I said. Then I realized I was standing barefoot on my mother's discarded blouse.

"'You should be in bed,' she said.

"Then Big Red started chortling. 'Little fella,' he laughed, 'take a good look at your Mama's titters.'

"Then he pinched Mother's behind, which made her angry, more angry at Red than at me, of course, but Mother's anger, like so much anger, was never neatly targeted in its assault.

"'You shut up,' Mother said to Red, then swung her face back around toward me. 'And you get back to bed.'

"Her yellow teeth were clenched.

"'I need a water,' I said again.

"'I'll bring you the damned water,' she said. Then she rose and swiped something off the kitchen counter and slapped it into my small palms. Mother was always giving gifts with her orders; "payoffs," my brother Frank would say years later, shaking his head, "guilt-reducing bribes," he would explain, raising an eyebrow.

"I rolled the colorful, cardboard cylinder with my fingertips and then looked up at Mother.

"'It's a kaleidy-scope,' she explained. 'Now get back to bed. I'll bring your water, baby. And we'll just pretend like none of this ever happened.'

"Mother smiled sweetly.

"Pretend, I thought. Pretend."

Pretend.

Buck is smiling now, giving me his don't-worry-your-pretty-little-head, we'll-find-some-way-to-get-you-out-of-this smile.

"He's gotten even worse than he was a few days ago," Stuart says about me, as if I'm not even there, man, as if I can't even hear these knife words that stab and twist into me like some back alley execution.

What about love, I say to myself. What about hope?

But, of course, I knew yesterday there was no love. I realized yesterday there was no hope. Two days ago I was flying high on hope.

But yesterday was The Day After. Yesterday, I got to thinking.

And, yesterday, reality came a knockin', in the personage of a *different* volunteer—not Stuart—from the agency. "Well," I remember thinking, "Stuart could never love a guy like me."

"A guy like me"—Jesus, listen to that.

"Well," says Jody, just to make things worse, "Roy's been out all night. I'm sure he hasn't eaten or taken any medicine."

Buck kneels, leans close. "Roy," he says, "can you hear me?"

When I don't answer—how do you answer something like that anyway?—Buck speaks in a louder, firmer voice. "Roy," he snaps, "can you *hear* me?"

When I still don't answer, he looks disappointed so I say, "Yes." But instead of cheering them, the hoarse brittleness of my voice makes them all the more uneasy.

From somewhere in my mind I hear another voice, the old leather voice of Marine Sergeant Pablo Luiz. "Get The Picture, Son," he snarls. "Keep A Grip On Things, Son . . . Obey, Son, Obey . . . Mind If I Put My Hand Here?"

"why no sir, not at all."

Semper fi, I think.

La vida es corta, I think. Yes, Sergeant Luiz, you taught me those words: *La vida es corta, y la muerte larga.*

You taught me those words that morning—yes, *that* morning.

The morning when you said, "Mind If I Put My Hand Here?" The morning when, later, just after the explosion, you fumbled with your belt buckle, saying, "Pretend nothing happened. Pretend nothing happened."

The morning we came running from the back of the compound to learn that a suicide-terrorist truck bomber had just plowed through the gates and blown 283 of our best buddies to bits.

The morning the two of us stood there, cringing, our faces flushed from fast sex, Middle East heat and, now, this—a high-sky fire explosion that made chips of bone and flesh dance high toward the heavens and fall back to Earth like tiny, ashen snowflakes.

That morning.

"*La vida es corta*," you mumbled, as we both stared at the flames, "*y la muerte larga.*"

Then you looked at me and scowled. "Remember," you growled. "Nothing happened." And then you ran away from me. Adios.

Well, something did happen, Sergeant. Excuse me, sir, but I find I must beg to differ.

Something happened then—and something happened when I returned home. When I returned home, I was a victim of another sort of terrorist attack. But this time there've been no big explosions.

Just slow death, this time.

Slow . . . slow . . . slow death.

And, this time, I cannot pretend.

Maple Park.

The old man has grown quite tired. His words come slower now.

"Sitting beside me on my bed," the old man says, "with her blouse back on but mis-buttoned quickly, my mother was trying to smile. She watched as I swallowed a sip of water, then cautioned, 'Not too much, honey, or you'll be up all night peeing. All finished?'

"I nodded and she grasped the glass and kissed my forehead again. 'Now sweet dreams,' she said.

"'Goodnight,' I said, then remembered the cardboard cylinder which I had brought into bed with me. 'What's this, Mom?'

"As fast as she rose, she flashed me a wide smile.

"'I told you,' she said. 'It's a kaleidy-scope. It's a little something your Uncle Red bought me. Isn't it nice? Wasn't it nice of your Uncle Red to do that?'

"Red was, in fact, my Uncle—my dead father's younger brother. After my father drove his car into a ditch, his family had talked my mother into moving out of the city—'so the boys can still be close to their loved ones,' is the way one sentence reads in a brief letter Red himself penned to my mother.

"'What's a kaleidy-scope?' I asked.

"'You look through it,' Mother replied, 'and see magic. Now get some sleep.'

"With that, Mother blew me another quick kiss, took a quick look at Frank still asleep in his crib nearer the window and closed the door on us. Frank was, is, a deep sleeper. I have always been more than a little restless, curious about the noisy adult world that seemed to pass me by each and every evening. So in the darkness of the bedroom, I raised the kaleidoscope to me eye as if I were lifting a prize—but I saw nothing.

"'Magic,' I sniffed, but then I tried again.

"I leveled the cylinder to my right eye and closed my left eye tightly. I saw nothing. I twisted the tip of the cylinder, around and around. But I still saw nothing. I was just about to give up when an image appeared: a big, bright, beautiful red explosion. And then another image appeared: Uncle Red, naked from the waist down. Moving away, standing apart from my mother. Facing me, bobbing with laughter.

"'Magic,' I said and pulled the toy under my covers and closed both my eyes to listen to the mysteries of the night."

Magic.

I lift my head weakly, look at their three sad faces: Buck and Jody and Stuart—dear Stuart, sweet Stuart, *my* Stuart . . . fuck Stuart.

I lift my head weakly and say in the voice they hate to hear: "One day," I say. "One day, man, a man wakes up and realizes there is no more mystery, no more love, no more hope, no more nothing from nobody.

"One day, man, a man wakes up and says, 'God, please, get-me-the-fuck-outta-here' and, in a dizzy-spinny daze he stumbles out of the apartment the agency rents for him . . . he staggers away from the pills and food the agency buys for him . . . he turns tail and walks away from all his so-called Friends and Loved Ones—and this man, man, he stumbles across the park, bumping into walls, bumping into people, bumping into their happy-sappy golden retrievers—and they just sidestep him or maybe even mumble, 'Fuck off, buddy,' but this man, man, he mumbles, 'Fuck off, buddy,' too, because he's fucked and he's been fucked and he's your worst nightmare: He's *you*, man, and you know it.

"So one day, man, this man collapses on the rocks along the lakeshore and he thinks. He thinks: 'I'm just a bug, man. End of story.'

"'Oh, no,' you might say. 'I—*I*—think you're much more than just a bug. I—*I*—believe you are a Human Being.'

"But this man, man, he just has to laugh.

"'Don't laugh,' you might say. 'I—*I*—am quite serious. I—*I*—am Aware. *I* am Compassionate. *I* care about my Fellow Man.'

"But this man, man, he just laughs and laughs.

"'You,' the man explains, 'give twenty bucks to a hospice. You tell your friends at dinner parties, "This epidemic must be stopped!" Maybe you even wear a handsome red ribbon, man.

"'But I,' the man continues, '*I* have become invisible through your feel-good awareness. *I* don't need your simple compassion. *I* need your courage—because mine's almost all gone. And I don't need you to care. *I* need your outrage—because you're about to bury mine with me.'

"'But but,' you might interrupt. 'I give you my courage. You have my outrage.'

"And the man only smiles. 'Oh, really?' he asks. 'Let's see how you feel when you catch me necking with your son.'"

Amen.

The old man tells you he has grown tired of talking. Outside, the sun is setting.

The old man says, "But there is still more to this story. You see," the old man continues, "I kept that kaleidoscope for years. And every time I looked through it, in light or dark, I'd see the big, bright, beautiful explosion and then Big Red standing there naked, bobbing at me with his overalls and underwear bunched around his ankles. And I was ever so protective of that kaleidoscope—I'd never, never ever, let Frank play with it.

"'It's all mine,' I'd scream, even when Frank pushed me, even when Frank cried.

"It was unlike me to be so uncharitable, even as a child. But I was afraid, you see. Fear has always been my motivator. I was afraid that if Frank looked through my kaleidoscope, he'd see what I saw—and he'd know my secret.

"The years passed. There was never anything serious between Mother and Uncle Red . . . 'Serious.' Listen to that . . . Red ended up marrying some girl from DeKalb and my mother ended up turning to the 'big loves' in our little town: God and Country. Every night, she took to reading the Bible to me and Frank, and then, every night before I went to bed, she'd talk to me about how she couldn't wait for the day to see me wearing the pressed uniform of the United States Marines.

"Then one afternoon in my last year of high school, Mrs. Baines caught me behind her house with one of the Martinez twins. I had my blue jeans undone. Mrs. Baines didn't yell at us, but she did tell us to go home. I remember her words exactly. 'Boys,' she said. 'Your business is your business and I won't tell your mothers. But you both best be getting on home for supper.'

"Mrs. B was true to her word—but, my little brother Frank was less understanding. He had come looking for me and he caught Mrs. Baines catching Felix Martinez and me.

"I got home just as Frank got home and Frank went straight to Mother.

"I cringed with the thought of what Frank was saying, so I hurried into my bedroom. Through the wall, all I could hear was 'on his knees.' Even then, I knew a death sentence when I heard one, and a moment later, Mother burst into my room and cracked my face with her open palm.

"'Stay away from those Martinez boys,' she screamed and I started crying. Then she cracked me again. 'You stay away,' she shouted and when she raised her hand a third time I fell back against my nightstand. I grabbed something to defend myself.

"I grabbed the kaleidoscope. I whacked my mother just above her right eye, nicking her with the kaleidoscope's thin, tin edge.

"Mother stopped fighting then. She traced the small cut with the tips of her shaking fingers. When she saw her smeared blood, she started crying these big tears of shame. She slowly, calmly, pulled the kaleidoscope out of my hand—it remains the only gift she's ever taken back."

The old man sighs.

"Then," the old man says, "Mother turned and stepped toward the door. With her back to me and her free hand trembling on the door frame, I heard my mother speak, her voice just barely a whisper.

"'Let's just pretend,' she said, 'that none of this ever happened.'

"And that's exactly what we did. None of us—Mom, Frank, me—none of us ever once mentioned it again. And the next month, Mrs. Baines died. And the next month later, I joined the Marines."

The old man closes his eyes.

Mea culpa.

Buck leans toward me.

"Roy," he says. "You're in a bad way. We need to call an ambulance."

I shake my head.

"Roy," he snaps. "We *need* to call—"

Before he finishes I say: "Stuart. Stuart. Stuart, what do you think?"

The tears in Stuart's eyes now mix with surprise.

"What do I think about what?"

I swallow. "Do you love me Stuart?"

He looks pained. "I don't really know you," he says.

"Nobody knows anybody," I say. "Do you *love* me?"

No one says a word.

"I don't want you to die," Stuart says.

"Yes," I say. "But do you love me?"

All he can do is not look at me. "I don't even know you well enough," he says.

"'Well enough,'" I say. "'Well enough' . . . Well enough? . . . Well, enough . . . Enough."

Jody is crying, too. I think maybe the boy finally gets the picture. I look back at Buck.

"*Semper fi*," I say and he squeezes my hand.

"You are not alone," Buck says to me, but I know he's really saying these words to himself. He wants so much to believe them.

"Yes, I am," I say.

Buck squeezes my hand tighter.

"*La vida es corta*," I say. "You have no idea where you're going. Adios."

My eyes close and I picture Mother, sitting on the couch with curlers in her hair, Frank and me, children again, sitting on the floor. The TV is turned off. Only the table lamp beside my mother is lit.

She reads from the Bible.

> "And Cain talked with Abel his brother; and it came
> to pass, when they were in the field, that Cain rose
> up against Abel his brother, and slew him.

> "And the Lord said unto Cain, Where is Abel thy
> brother. And he said, I know not: Am I my brother's keeper?"

Amen, I think, Amen.

I am a man who likes to remember, I think, and now I'll never be the old man I always hoped to be, the old man telling stories in the autumn sunshine.

Instead, I am here—now—going, almost gone. I see nothing now, the same nothing I saw when I first looked through that kaleidoscope years and years and oh-so-many fucking years ago. There's no more mystery, no more magic. I see nothing. I know nothing. I feel nothing. I am—

A white-toothed boy rides through the park on his mountain bike and looks toward the lake and sees nothing but glistening bright blue sunshine glistening. "What a lovely day," he says.

Eddie Doyle Says Life's Been Good

__Blessed are the poor in spirit:__
__for theirs is the Kingdom of Heaven.__

"Did you hear about Jimmy?"

"No."

"Cracked his fucking head open."

"No!"

"Yeah—gash, blood, everything."

"Oh, Jesus."

"Right here. Last night. On the edge of the bar. It was Doyle who done it."

"Doyle? Doyle hit Jimmy?"

"No—"

"Eddie Doyle got into a fight with Jimmy Conklin?"

"No—listen, there wasn't no fight. It was just Doyle talking. Just Doyle talking so much, like he does, that he started boring Jimmy and Jimmy's head starting bobbing and dipping and dipping and bobbing and the next thing I see is Jimmy passing out and—boom!—popping his head right against the bar."

"Oh, Jesus!"

"Right off the bar, onto the floor."

"Jesus! That bicycle-seat Irish Doyle."

"Yeah, well, that's Dull Doyle for you. That's Dull Doyle all over."

__Blessed are they that mourn:__
__for they shall be comforted.__

Eddie Doyle frowned when he saw Tess, his daughter, still sitting at the round kitchen table in their small, dusty apartment. "No school?" he said.

"No school."

"Columbus Day or something?"

"No."

"What?"

The girl was reading the back of a cereal box as she ate with a spoon from a white bowl. She shrugged her slim shoulders and snatched long, straight hair away from hanging in her face. Doyle frowned again because he did not like the way his daughter kept her hair.

"Some sort of Institute Day, I guess," Tess mumbled.

"Oh," Doyle said. "They close that high school any chance they get, don't they?"

"Huh?" the girl said. "I guess."

"They make up holidays to close it."

"Yeah," the girl mumbled. She had not looked up. "Guess."

Eddie Doyle stuffed his cold hands into the big pockets of his tattered, faded, rose-colored robe. His thinning black hair was uncombed across the top of his head. His face was white when he looked at his daughter again. "You goin' out then?"

She swiped her hair again. "No."

"No?"

The girl shook her head. She was dressed in baggy jeans and a too-big, gray T-shirt. The girl kept reading the blue and yellow cereal box.

Eddie Doyle looked at the clock on the wall above the dishes piled in the sink. It was just past ten in the morning.

"Maybe you should go out," he said.

The girl kept eating and reading. She was hungry.

Eddie Doyle walked around the table to the stove and lit the gas burner beneath the silver metal tea kettle. "I guess I'll have some tea," he said. "You want some tea?"

The girl shook her head.

"Your mother," Eddie said, "she was always one for tea."

But Tess just kept eating and reading. Her mother had been dead for only a short time and Tess felt bad thinking of her. When she thought about her mother, she cried.

Eddie looked at the clock again and held his hands flat near the tea kettle for warmth. He smiled, suddenly, and turned off the burner.

"I guess maybe I should throw some clothes on and run down to the corner for smokes," he said.

Tess spoke with her mouth full of crunchy cereal. "There's a pack there," she said, pointing with her chin to the center of the kitchen table.

"Oh, yeah," Eddie said, seeing the Camels now. "Thanks." He re-lit the burner.

The girl grew tired of reading the cereal box and nudged it away. She looked into her bowl and began drawing the spoon more quickly to her mouth.

Eddie smiled again. "I better get the paper then," he said.

"Got it," the girl mumbled. "On the couch."

"You know," Eddie Doyle said sharply. He was no longer smiling. His hands were deep in his robe's pockets. "You know," he said, "I can *get* my own newspaper. I can *get* my own cigarettes. You don't have to *get* things for me. I can *get* my own things, you know."

His voice sounded like he wanted to start a fight.

"Yeah," Tess said, without turning. "Well," she said, without looking, "you can *get* your paper on the couch."

That really made Eddie angry. It was something his wife, Doreen, would have said. But Eddie did not really want to get angry with Tess. He shuffled into the darkened living room and picked up the *Sun-Times* from the couch. The musty drapes were still drawn across the picture window.

The girl called from the kitchen. "You know," she said, "if you want to go out and go by O'Brien's, you can. I know you do it, Dad. Some of the guys, on their way to school, they seen you and Jimmy go by O'Brien's this early in the morning. They asked me if it was you they seen."

The girl was then surprised to look up and see her father standing so close. His big face was turning red. His small eyes looked black beneath thin, arching eyebrows.

"I don't know those kids," Eddie Doyle said. His teeth were clenched. "And I don't know what they're talking about. I ain't been to O'Brien's, not in a long time. Not since your mother got sick. I don't want to go to O'Brien's now. So you can tell them, Tess, tell them it just wasn't me they saw. And you can stop talking to me in such a condensation tone."

Tess had to catch her breath and then she felt like laughing, but she did not laugh because she remembered her father once saying, without looking at her, that her laugh had reminded him of her mother's laugh. So all Tess did was catch her breath and say, "Sure." And then: "Sure, Dad. Sorry, Dad. Sure, I'll let them know they're wrong."

Blessed are the meek:
for they shall inherit the earth.

"Get this."

"Get what?"

"Doyle."

"Poor Eddie. You ought to lay off him . . . So?"

"So, you know how Doyle got that job at the store, down at the hardware, through his brother-in-law, Doreen's little brother, Frankie?"

"Yeah."

"Well, Doyle fucked it up."

"No—"

"Big time. The guy can't sell squat."

"Poor Eddie. What'd he do?"

"Fucked up. Real good. He's back to driving the cab. Started doing nutty right on the first day—blabbing on and on about Doreen when he should've been selling and then he starts balling—yeah, can you believe it? like a baby, right there in the store—and then he gets all embarrassed and starts mouthing off. Frankie, you know, Frankie's got a good business, he can't put up with that. Frankie, you know, he had no choice."

"What could he do?"

"Exactly. Business is business. Did what he had to do. Fired Doyle. His dead sister's husband, but—boom!—right there, in the middle of the store, with customers around and everything . . . You want another?"

"Poor Eddie . . . Sure. Yeah."

"A guy's got to believe in himself even if he don't believe in nothing else, but Doyle, well, Doyle don't believe in nothing."

Blessed are they which do hunger and thirst for righteousness: for they shall be filled.

It was near closing time at O'Brien's. Eddie Doyle sat at the bar beside Jimmy Conklin. Jimmy's right temple was taped with a once-white bandage.

"I'll tell you what I think," Eddie Doyle was saying. "I think the church is full of shit. I hate to say it, but it's true. First of all, all this kneeling. Hell, Jimmy, I'm too old to kneel. I can't kneel no more. I've knelt too much in my life, Jimmy."

Jimmy nodded and looked crookedly at the mirrored shelves of green and golden bottles stacked behind the bar. Jimmy was skinny and taller than Eddie, but when Jimmy's shoulders slumped, as they were slumping now, Eddie could look down on him.

"I lost my knees in the service, anyway," Eddie Doyle went on. "The service and sixty years of those goddamned wooden kneelers. But I'll tell you why else I think the church is cracked. Money. Money-money-money, Jimmy. Always wanting money. And not just at Mass. It's *always* with the hand out. The big hand right out there, palm up, in your face, reaching, grabbing, saying, '*Gimme.*' Saying, '*Gimme*—and be blessed, my son.' Saying, '*Gimme*—and ye shall be forgiven.' They put a price tag on hope and I bought it, Jimmy. I paid and paid for it—and nothing. Jimmy, I'm telling you: The church is nothing, a lousy business, filled with liars and cheats, that's all. They wear their collars, Jimmy, but they're worse than the congressmen. Worse than the aldermen, even. Doreen and I were talking about it just last night."

Jimmy Conklin blinked and cocked his head sharply. "Doreen?"

Eddie slurped foam off his freshly poured beer.

"She was sitting there at the kitchen table, smoking like always, nodding up and down like always," Doyle said. He laughed and shook his head. "Doreen says it's all nothing but superstition anyway. 'One man's faith,' she says, 'is another man's superstition.'"

Jimmy blinked again. "Doreen? But—"

"Worst part," Eddie Doyle continued. "I told Doreen the worst part. I told Doreen, 'Think of all the horrors that have been done in the name of the World's Great Superstitions. Think—'"

Eddie Doyle saw Jimmy's eyelids flutter and close. Eddie drank some beer as Jimmy's eyelids sprang open again, then, snapped shut. The skinny man's head dipped once, then twice before thwacking against the bar top.

"*Jesus*, Eddie!" The bartender shouted from down the bar. He threw a soggy rag into the small sink behind the bar and marched to where Jimmy had collapsed from his stool to the floor. The bartender leaned over the bar top, growling, "Doyle, you dull son of a bitch, you've *got* to watch what you're doing. Jimmy whacked his other side this time!"

Blessed are the merciful:
for they shall obtain mercy.

"The Doyle girl."

"What about her?"

"Tess."

"Yeah. Tess. What about her?"

"She's—you know, like this."

"No—who's the father?"

"Who knows? Some McKinley Park punk probably."

"How's Eddie taking it?"

"Eddie? He don't even know."

"He don't know?"

"She hasn't told him. Nobody's told him, so don't you go telling him. I just heard it from my Sheila, this morning."

"Poor Eddie."
"Yeah. Well, I say, fuck Eddie."

Blessed are the pure in heart:
for they shall see God.

Eddie Doyle tried smiling. Tess was sitting at the kitchen table, eating well-cooked eggs and plain bread.

"Morning," Eddie Doyle said, putting his hands into the pockets of his robe. "Happy Thanksgiving."

The girl did not look up. "Yeah," she mumbled, between bites. "Happy Thanksgiving."

Eddie Doyle frowned a little. He was looking at Tess and thinking of Doreen. Plus, he always felt sore in the mornings now. Sore and dry.

"Hey," he said, his face brightening. "How 'bout a little shot of something? A Thanksgiving toast."

He was grinning now, pleased with himself and moving eagerly to the cupboard above the sink.

"A Thanksgiving toast," Eddie explained. "My father and I—we *always* started off Thanksgiving Day with a toast."

Eddie took down two heavy glasses and a bottle of Bushmill's.

"Ah," Tess said, "I better pass."

"Huh? No, just a little shot."

Eddie turned to face Tess. He was thinking now of his father and Doreen and Tess and Thanksgiving and all of the Thanksgiving days and the whiskey and Doreen and Tess and how she smiled as a baby and how someday—

"No thanks, Dad," the girl said softly. "Really, Dad," she said, "you go ahead. Happy Thanksgiving." She was trying hard not to start a fight. "Thanks anyway. I just don't have a taste for it," she said and stood. "I'll cook us a big dinner later. Sit down now. You have your toast—and I'll fix you some breakfast."

Tess tried smiling and reached across the kitchen table and touched her father's hand.

Blessed are the peacemakers:
for they shall be called the children of God.

"Forgive me, Father, for I have sinned. It's been a long time, you know, since I ever confessed..."

"Yes, Eddie. I'm glad you're back."

"I'm sorry, Father . . . I got no business being here . . . I—"

"Just talk to me, Eddie."

"Father, I . . . I—"

"Yes, Eddie, go on . . ."

"I'm not one to complain, Father. Don't get me wrong. My life's been pretty okay. I'm not one of those guys, Father, who goes around croaking about all his trials and tributaries."

". . . Yes, Eddie. Go on."

"Well, it's Doreen, Father. I know she's supposed to be gone. I know she's supposed to be gone and everything, but I still talk. . . . Sometimes I still see . . ."

"Go on."

"Father—"

"Go on, Eddie."

"But that's just it, Father . . . There's nothing left . . . I'm not sure I can go on."

Blessed are they which are persecuted for righteousness' sake: for theirs is the Kingdom of Heaven.

After midnight, Eddie Doyle unlocked his front door and staggered inside.

Tess looked up from the living room couch. She was curled beneath a gray quilt, watching TV in the dark. The TV screen glimmered with old men dressed in resplendent red robes and slippers celebrating High Mass in Rome. The air around them was clouded with wisps of smoke.

Eddie stumbled indoors, pressing his palms flat against the wall to gain balance. He gave the front door a swift but unsteady kick closed.

Tess was now used to seeing her father like this, but she felt a chill when Eddie mumbled, "Baby."

He turned to face his daughter on the couch. He squinted into the darkness and stepped forward. "I miss you, Baby," he said.

Tess' face was in the bluish TV light, but Eddie was looking passed her, through her. Tess put a hand on her stomach and thought of her mother and felt like crying.

Then she saw that Eddie had been crying, too. "I miss you, Baby," Eddie sobbed once more.

"*Dad,*" Tess snapped sharply as if she were trying to awaken him.

Her father fell to his knees by the door and groaned and wept. "God-damn everything," he mumbled.

Tess pushed the warm quilt onto the floor, rushed to her father and knelt beside him. He was trembling and smelled of beer. Tess slowly reached a thin arm around her father's round shoulders. "Dad," she whispered. "I miss her, too."

*Blessed are ye, when men shall revile you, and persecute you,
and shall say all manner of evil against you falsely, for my sake.*

The next morning, Eddie Doyle sat on the edge of his bed, inhaled deeply, stretched his arms above his head and yawned. He felt refreshed. He looked at the morning sun shinning white against the drawn window shade and then stood and grabbed his robe from the foot of the bed. His hands were cold and his knees were sore, but that no longer bothered him. He carefully put on his robe and dipped his hands far into the pockets. He shut his eyes and stood very still for a long time. Then Eddie Doyle smelled cigarette smoke. He smiled, inhaled deeply again, opened his eyes, reached for the bedroom door and stepped into the kitchen.

Doreen was wearing her pink-colored robe, sitting at the kitchen table with her legs crossed, smoking. She turned and looked at Eddie Doyle calmly, without smiling.

"Baby!" Doyle said and rushed to her and kissed her cheek, but she did not move and her cheek was ice cold. But Eddie was still smiling. "Baby!" he shouted again. He put his hands on Doreen's shoulders, but her shoulders, even through her thick robe, felt bony and delicate. "It's great to see you, Baby," he said again.

Tess stepped into the kitchen from her bedroom to find her father gripping the back of an empty, white, wooden kitchen chair. His knuckles were white. "Dad?" Tess said. Her voice was faint and scared.

Eddie Doyle turned quickly. He grinned broadly. His eyes sparkled. "Morning, Tess," he said loudly. "Tess, look who's here. Say good morning, Tess. Wish your mother a Merry Christmas."

Amen

The last time Neal Casey saw Father Daniel the old priest was three days away from death. Father Daniel was stretched out in a cramped, but sunny room at St. Agnes and Neal Casey recognized deeply and all at once that the small priest did not look happy to see him—a realization that was not altogether unpleasant for Neal Casey.

"Shut the lousy blinds," Father Daniel wheezed as his visitor stepped inside the doorway. "Couldn't get a nurse in here if your life depended on it."

Neal Casey slowly walked around the foot of Father Daniel's white hospital bed to the window. He pulled three different narrow cords before he figured out which one closed the thin metal blinds. He watched as slender strips of afternoon sunlight faded into a shadow across Father Daniel's skinny, colorless face.

"Not the nurses' fault," the priest continued in a low grumble, as if Neal Casey might be just any visitor. "It's the louts—forgive me for saying so—running this place who really are to blame."

Neal Casey stood very straight and still and said hello.

The priest squinted to bring his visitor into full focus: Neal Casey's apple face, red and chubby, his wide neck pinched tight within a buttoned white collar and burgundy tie. Father Daniel nodded and smiled slightly then. The collar was never a comfortable fit for either man.

The two Southsiders went way back. Father Daniel had married Neal Casey to Helen. He had baptized Neal and Helen's two daughters. He had attended the girls' communions and confirmations, as well. He had given last rites to Neal Casey's mother—and then, one week later, last rites to Neal Casey's father, too. Over the years, Neal Casey must have stood before Father Daniel more than a thousand times and looked into the priest's watery blue eyes to hear him intone, "The body of Christ . . ." and to hear himself reply, "Amen."

But, this was the first time in a long time that Neal Casey had seen Father Daniel face-to-face. Both men felt the knot of years and silence in their stomachs.

"If the Church hadn't stopped listening to me," Father Daniel continued, groaning slightly as he squirmed to half-sit against the flattened pillows in his bed, "this old place wouldn't be in any of the trouble she's in. Now, there's no hope of saving her." He waved his arms out to his sides as if he was still talking and then let his hands drop.

Father Daniel's visitor removed his heavy gray overcoat, folded it over his left arm and stepped closer to the bed. Father Daniel looked up at Neal and then away toward the blinds. Both men remained silent until the priest asked, "And how are the girls?"

Neal Casey said his daughters were fine.

"Married?" Father Daniel's voice carried little genuine interest.

Neal Casey said the eldest married about seven years ago, only to divorce four years later. Neal Casey added, with a warm smile, that the youngest was just engaged this past Christmas.

Father Daniel nodded sharply, then, glanced again at his visitor.

"And Helen," the priest said, his voice softening, his eyes opening wider with the memories. "How is our Helen?"

Neal Casey cleared his throat, loosened his tie and unbuttoned his collar. *Our* Helen. Neal had anticipated that Father Daniel would provoke him, but he was committed to not surrendering to his years of anger. Instead, he simply told Father Daniel that Helen was fine.

"Yes," Father Daniel said and smiled. Neal Casey had expected the smile, too—thin and stretching across the man's gaunt face. When the old priest's smile passed, Father Daniel said: "I'm dying. You know, don't you? I'm dying. In fact, when you first arrived I thought you might be Death Himself coming for me."

Neal Casey sighed and looked toward the door. He said he knew. He said, in fact, it was this news that had motivated him to visit. He refrained from adding how he had told no one, save Helen, about his intention to visit. Nor did he explain his almost comical dodging of the one or two nurses he passed in the mostly empty hospital corridors to reach the priest in room 435.

Father Daniel was still looking at Neal Casey.

The two men were roughly the same age. They had both boxed in high school. They had both been in the Army, both drafted during Korea. After the service, Neal Casey returned to Chicago, to McKinley Park, and met Helen. Father Daniel headed farther north, to Minnesota and the seminary. A few years later, Father Daniel came back home.

"We've grown old," Father Daniel said. "I suppose we all three of us have white hair now."

Neal Casey nodded and looked at his shiny black shoes. He found himself recalling a younger, thinner, dark-haired Helen. A different Helen. *But I love you*, he was saying to her, tears smeared across both of their faces. *Yes*, she was replying as she sat on their bed, an empty red hat box opened upon her lap. *You love me. But love is not enough*, she was saying. *Can you forgive me?*

"It is difficult to imagine Helen with white hair," Father Daniel added and Neal Casey heard the smile return to the old priest's voice.

"You should sit," Father Daniel continued, glancing around the small hospital room before growling. His voice was now more windy than forceful. "Can you believe there's not even a chair? Who thinks you don't need a chair for visitors? I can't believe how they have crippled this poor hospital. Nothing but ruins now."

Neal Casey said he was fine standing. He allowed the priest a minute to calm down.

The two men lived in a Southside neighborhood that went way back, too. Father Daniel had persuaded the old Cardinal, the Good Cardinal, to keep open the parish when the archdiocese was closing parishes left and right. The priest also had organized some businessmen years ago to throw some money into fortifying St. Agnes. In those days, there was even talk of building a new women's wing. Father Daniel had worked with Helen on starting a Ladies Auxiliary to help raise funds.

"Helen," Father Daniel said absently. He looked at his small, spotty hands tugging and pressing the creases of his white bed sheet. He waited for Neal Casey's eyes to meet his. "Does Helen still wear the hat I bought for her?"

Neal Casey shifted his weight onto one foot and shuffled his overcoat across his other arm. With his free hand, he gripped the bed rail. He kept himself from blinking.

Father Daniel was referring to a red hat with a narrow, black velvet band around its brim. The priest had given the hat as a gift to Helen on a spring weekend many, many years before.

"No," Neal Casey explained. "We got rid of the hat right away."

And then Neal Casey remembered he had forgotten the flowers. "Damn," he mumbled. "Helen had asked if she could pick some flowers from our garden—"

"—The garden around the bedroom?"

"No. The pretty one. The garden out front. Tulips," Neal Casey said. "She picked them and asked me to bring them, but I've left them on the kitchen table."

Father Daniel was no longer looking at Neal Casey.

Neal Casey found himself wondering if the priest was lost in the memories of shame, the pain of illness, or the promise of faith. Neal Casey shifted his weight back to his other foot and cleared his throat once again. The priest coughed, too, a heavy cough from deep inside his hollow chest. Neal Casey listened as the priest's cough echoed out of his lungs and around the room and into the long hallway.

"The louts," Father Daniel growled again as his coughing subsided. "They won't give me enough of anything to kill this coughing."

Neal Casey was once more looking at his shoes and after a while he told Father Daniel he had to leave. The two men glanced at one another and then Father Daniel grabbed Neal Casey's hand on the bedrail. Neal Casey had never before felt flesh as cold.

"I can't thank you enough for coming," Father Daniel said.

"Well," Neal Casey said. "I just didn't—"

Father Daniel squeezed Neal Casey's hand between his palms.

"No. Really. Thank you."

Neal Casey bit his lower lip and could not bring himself to look at the priest's blue eyes, now brimming with tears. "Well," Neal Casey said again. "Yes," he said. "I—it's more for me than any of the three of us, really. It's been a long, long time."

"Thank you," Father Daniel repeated.

"Well," Neal Casey said once more. "Yes . . ."

Finally, Father Daniel let go of Neal Casey's hand.

Three days later Neal Casey came across Helen sobbing beside the telephone in their bedroom. Father Daniel was dead. Three months later, the Church closed St. Agnes. Three months more and they tore the old place down.

No More

I wake up thinking what I always wake up thinking: I can't take any more of this.

Julio is beside me, naked, curled around his pillow. The sheets are bunched at our feet. The sun is just breaking through the metal blinds, but it's already too hot, too humid to touch.

I wake up coughing, and when I finally stop coughing I light a smoke, take a drag. I have a taste for coffee, too, but I want my coffee in my own place. I always want to be alone in the morning.

I cough again, enough to make me sit up, but not enough to make Julio wake up. We hit it pretty hard last night and I'm sure Julio won't open his eyes for hours. He has brown eyes, tired eyes.

I brush my thumb along the smoothness of his slender lower back and watch the tiny goose bumps rise. Even in this heat a human touch is still enough to make a man shiver.

Julio stirs and I laugh softly. I think about putting on my jeans, walking downstairs to my room, and making a pot of coffee.

Instead, I tickle Julio's goose bumps with my finger tips, which makes him squeeze his pillow tighter. Then I lean sideways and kiss his back. He moans as he stirs, and I kiss him once again, only lower.

"*No más,*" he murmurs, pushing my head away with his hand. Julio's eyes are still closed.

Downstairs at the cramped front desk, dressed, and drinking my second cup of coffee, I shake my head about Julio. I know he's a bad idea. I've known this now for weeks. I've known this since the first time he pressed himself against me and called me cowboy.

"I'm no cowboy," I told him. "I'm from New Orleans."

"But I like cowboys," he complained and kissed me fast. "And cowboys like me," he said and smiled widely.

Julio was drunk that night, like almost every night, like almost everyone always is at this Uptown hotel. Of course, I had not been drinking.

I never drink when I'm working, even though no one would ever know, and even if someone knew, they would never care. But for the three months I've worked the front desk at this SRO, not drinking on duty is the one promise I've kept. I've lied to cops and social workers about who comes and goes. I've let prostitutes use the rooms. I've even stolen a total of four dollars and thirty-five cents from the cash drawer. But I've always been sober.

"This is no job for a young man," my boss, Mr. Whistler, has told me. "Beggars, pimps, addicts, whores, pushers, con men, crooks. This job will turn your short hairs gray and make you an old man fast."

Mr. Whistler is over six foot tall. He's skinny and he wheezes and I knew the moment I met him that he'd seen it all.

This afternoon, I have to telephone the police. Just after two o'clock somebody upstairs fires a shotgun.

At first, I think about running upstairs to face the trouble, but when I don't hear another shot or any other sound, I get scared. Silence always makes me nervous.

Two patrolmen eventually show up. They wait for a third before they walk upstairs. In the few minutes they're gone, I actually switch channels for TV news to see if I can somehow find myself on a broadcast even though no reporters are present.

Finally, the third cop shuffles back downstairs. He's an old cop with a neat mustache and he looks like he's seen it all, as well. He's walking easy, but breathing hard.

"Face lift," he says.

"What?" I turn down the TV volume, even though I clearly heard what he said.

"Suicide," the cop explains. "Some old guy in 3-F. Got a name?"

"My name is Wayne," I tell him, and he frowns.

The cop speaks very slowly. "Got a name for the man with no face in 3-F? Old-timer, by the looks of things."

I feel stupid and my mind goes blank. I tell the cop I don't know, but I'll look it up. I turn my back, start flipping the wide pages of the resident register.

"Hell of a mess," the cop says behind me.

I draw my finger down the list of names, flip a few more pages.

"I hate suicides," the cop is saying. "This one at least left a note."

My finger stops at the name on line 3-F: Marvin H. Whistler. I turn to tell the cop it's Mr. Whistler.

"No more," the cop says.

"What?"

"'No more,'" he says again. "That's what the guy scribbled for his note. 'No more.'"

Suicides. Accidental deaths. Death by natural causes.

I've seen them all in these past three months. No murders yet, but this evening—it's a really hot night with a big white moon hanging over us almost like a threat—a fat guy staggers into our lobby stabbed in his back. But he doesn't die. I call the cops and my cop friend with the neat mustache comes again, and this time we actually save one.

Tonight, in bed, I'm thinking about Mr. Whistler. I ask Julio if he's afraid of death and he just shakes his head. "Kiss me," he says. He's drunk again. "Kiss me and shut up."

I ask how he manages to survive from day to day.

Julio groans. He rests his slender left arm across his eyes. "You know how I survive," he mumbles.

"But—why?" I ask. "Why do you go on surviving?"

Julio again shakes the tight, black, shaggy curls of his head and laughs. He reaches out to place his hand on my chest—because, I think, I'm getting too close.

"I used to have ambition," Julio says, looking right into my eyes. "But my old man beat that out of me. So then I had to rely on luck. But my luck kept changing. So that left me with faith."

Julio pauses, slips his hand onto my shoulder. He pulls us together. His skin is sticky. "But, baby," he mumbles again. "After all I've seen, after all I've done, I pray there's no God. And that leaves me with no faith. So all I've got now is hope. Just hope. Just hope—and, well, you."

Before I moved to Chicago, before I met Julio or Mr. Whistler, before I got this job, I had high hopes.

I was living with my eldest sister just outside of New Orleans, and I had dreams. But, in time, I was too much trouble for my sister and her family so I headed north to Baton Rouge and then farther north to here.

My sister and I did not part on the best of terms, but during the past few months I've still had enough guts to telephone her a few times. Late at night, on the old pay phone in the downstairs hallway, I've stood in darkness and dialed her number. Each time, I've asked my sister to tell me the same exact story: her memory of our mother, who died when I was four and my sister was eleven.

Tonight is one of those nights. I get out of bed without waking Julio. I tug on my jeans, step into the hall, walk downstairs and telephone my sister.

"Mama was a poor woman," my sister's voice says to me from 900 miles away. "Mama was an uneducated woman. Mama was a strict woman at times."

I close my eyes as my sister speaks. Her voice is full of warm sleep.

"Mama never left Louisiana," she whispers. "Mama never owned a television. Mama never read a newspaper. She only plugged in and played the radio on Saturdays."

I stand as close to the pay phone as I can.

"When Mama died in the big hospital, I was at her bedside," my sister explains. "And I remember Mama's words. 'No more,' she whispered. It wasn't that Mama had had enough of her pain, though I'm sure she had. It was that Mama, who was forever grateful to have married her husband, to have raised her children, to have made her home, to have lived life—Mama died wanting nothing more from life. She passed away content."

During these past three months, my sister and I have shared little other conversation. I say little else now. I tell her thanks and let her know I love her. She whispers that she loves me, too, and we hang up. Not including this call tonight, these long-distance memories have cost me four dollars and thirty-five cents.

Back in bed, Julio is naked and curled around his pillow.

"Cowboy," he murmurs, his eyes still shut. "You back in bed?"

I lie down beside him and once again embrace a bad idea.

All the Good Days

1.

Our faces (mine and those of my two nephews) are reddened and sweaty by the time we lift the torn, worn sofa bed off the back of the rented trailer. We grunt on the concrete steps, trying to make the turn and the turn again at the top of the steps to head across the breezeway to my new apartment.

I remember when this place was a two-story motel, built the year before my oldest nephew was born, and I remember when the motel closed down (the first time June and I separated). I stayed here that night, for one night, until the Pakistani manager pulled me aside and said, *Sorry, mister. We're closing. You've got to leave.*

Sometimes, it seems, all I do is leave.

—*Boy*, I say now as we drop (and I do mean drop) the old sofa bed in the middle of the tile floor, in the middle of my new home surrounded by boxes and wooden crates and things moved but not packed: folding chairs, the electric fan from the garage workbench, a bathroom trash basket stuffed with one roll of paper towels and two white extension cords.

—*Boys*, I say. *What do you say we crack open some beers?*

—*Oh, thanks no*, they say. *We should be going.* They're smiling. These boys are always smiling. *We really should be going.*

And they rub their young backs and my oldest nephew says he must get home to his new wife and my youngest nephew says he has yet another friend to move this afternoon.

—*But boys,* I say. *Just one beer. To say thanks, thanks for a job well-done.*

—*Oh, thanks no,* they say again, still smiling. *We really should be going.* And they go.

2.

The gas man comes just as I pop-top my third beer. He's a solid-looking man, with a thick, brown work belt, standing silhouetted in my open front door.

—*Gas man!* he shouts and even though I'm seeing him when he shouts, I jump and laugh and say, *Come in, come in.*

He comes in.

—*I know this place,* he says. *Won't take a minute.* And he steps over a ripped cardboard box stuffed with my clothes.

—*Just moved today,* I explain as Gas Man maneuvers around me, into the kitchenette, straight into the small pantry where he uses some tool to crank on the meter. *Hey, you want a beer?*

—*The old lady who lived here before you,* Gas Man says, shaking his head. *I turned off her gas when they finally put her in the nursing home. She hated it here. The roaches and the kid downstairs. Always with his drums. The old lady, she was really happy to leave.*

I swallow some beer and Gas Man starts in on the stove, lighting burners and the oven pilot. A grimy oven knob pops off into his hand and he holds it out toward me, at me, like an artifact or like evidence. Exhibit A.

—*You didn't check this place out,* Gas Man says. *Did you?*

I shrug and drink some beer.

On his hands and knees now, Gas Man reaches under my furnace and lights that pilot, too.

—*The old lady,* he says. *She also said there was always a lot of screaming.* Then, Gas Man looks up at me.

—*Listen,* I tell him. My teeth are clenched. *Don't you tell me about ghosts.*

3.

The first telephone call I receive comes later that evening. The phone rings and I jump and pick up the receiver saying, *June, honey? June?*

—*Ah,* a young man says. *Your phone: It's finally working.* Then he calls me by name and there is no more "ah" in his voice.

—*This is Mr. Winnick,* he continues. *I am Mr. Winnick of Carp and Winnick, and your wife has given me your number and has advised me to settle this matter with you. This is a matter of several unpaid medical bills, sir, including an unpaid radiologist's bill, outstanding now for more than seven months, sir, for more than seven months. The matter has been turned over to our firm for collection and legal action if legal action is necessary, sir. We ask that you avoid legal action by making payment today. Can you do that, sir? Will you make payment today, make payment now?*

I say nothing.

—*Do you know, sir, do you have any idea of how serious a matter this is?*

This kid, this Winnick, he certainly sounds serious.

—*If,* he continues. *If you do not pay today, if you do not pay now, we will be forced to proceed with legal action. With legal action, sir. Sir?*

Again, I say nothing.

—*Sir,* the kid continues. *I do not believe you fully, truly, really understand. I do not think you understand the seriousness involved, sir.*

I find I still have nothing to say.

—*You obviously do not understand,* the kid says.

—*I,* I say, but the kid hangs up.

Then I hang up, too. I hang up hard and kick a small box out of my way as I return to the fridge.

This is a good day's work for that kid, I tell myself.

I then realize I've finished all of the beer so I slam hard the refrigerator door, too.

This is what that kid does, I tell myself. This is how this Winnick earns his living. This: He breaks and enters into another guy's life. He accuses the guy of not understanding when really there is too much for anyone to understand. And then? And then this Winnick calls it a day. He calls it a day and probably stops for a beer with a buddy and they laugh together about the good day they have had and all the good days they have ever had ever. And they laugh and drink beer and eye some girls and laugh some more.

So I drop onto my old sofa bed and stare up at my new ceiling, the only uncluttered part of my new home. And I wish I had just one more beer to help me sleep now and when the telephone rings again, I let it ring. I let it ring and ring.

I let the telephone ring because I am too busy to answer. Too busy listening. Listening for those screams that will come in the night.

Together

At times like this—when our youngest daughter gets wet-eyed, tight-faced angry with her mother and me, when she makes hard fists from her little hands and stomps upstairs to her big bedroom and sprawls across the soft pillows of her wide, white bed, sobbing, "Nobody loves me, nobody loves me"—my wife catches me coming close to losing my temper and she tells me to remember.

She means I should remember Jewels. Jewels and the summers of my life from two dozen summers ago.

I met Jewels when I was eighteen years old, working my first night as a host at a Near North restaurant. The tuxedo I wore and the tenacity I showed were both on loan: the tuxedo, borrowed, until I could afford to purchase one; the tenacity, rented, from my father who had suddenly told me, "From now on, you're on your own. Get a job like everyone else. Get an apartment like everyone else. Good-bye. Good luck. You'll need it."

On my first night as a restaurant host—the first real night of my new life—three guys in navy suits and yellow ties bolted from their table without paying. Trying to impress my new boss, as well as my new self, with my brave new maturity, I naturally did the very wrong thing: I ran onto the street after them.

They barreled passed in a roaring Buick LeSabre, nearly running me down. Their car was followed by a black Lincoln Continental, which screeched to a halt before me. The Lincoln's shadowed passenger window lowered silently, automatically, to reveal a female driver.

"What's the problem, darling?"

"Those guys just bolted," I said.

"Well," the woman said. "Don't you think you better get in?"

Without thinking, I opened the passenger door and leaped inside. Before I closed the door, she floored the accelerator.

"Can't stand cheaters," she said. "Particularly punk cheaters. My name's Jewels."

I looked across the seat at her—at this woman with silver-white hair, this not-pretty, not-unattractive older woman who wore silver rings and a black-and-silver evening dress and smoked a Pall Mall. I couldn't help but smile.

"Pardon me?" I said.

"Jewels," she said. "J-E-W-E-L-S. There are your boys."

She slammed on the brakes and we skidded to a stop right behind the Buick, which was idling at a red light. I could see the three of them—big guys, slicked-back hair—laughing, slapping each other on the back, celebrating the great success of their monumental caper. I looked again at this woman.

"What do I do now?" I said.

Jewels faced me and gave me the slowest, most drawn-out look of disappointment—and the worst kind of disappointment, too, the kind shaded by pity. Indeed, this was a look I would come to know too well.

"Well," she said, "it's *your* chase, darling."

"But I can't very well just go up to them and ask them to nicely pay this bill, to just let—"

I never finished because the light turned green, the Buick jumped forward and Jewels stamped the accelerator again. She moved bumper-to-bumper with the offenders and flashed her sweeping headlights off-on, off-on, off-on. I saw the backs of their heads, then their surprised faces, then their shocked faces—eyebrows up, six eyes opened wide.

Jewels swung her big car around to their left and yelled passed me to their driver: "Lousy cheats. Punk cheats. Your days are numbered!"

Their car swerved to the right and hightailed down a side street. Jewels watched them escape in her rear-view mirror.

"Chicken punks," she snarled, slowing her car for another red light. She tilted her head toward me. "Did you at least get their license plate?"

I didn't say a word.

"Darling?"

I kept my mouth shut.

I shook my head slowly.

As we slowed to a stop, Jewels gave me another long look of disappointment-pity, then, broke out the warmest smile I have ever seen. Her baby blue eyes shimmered. "Not to worry, darling. Jewels got it. What'd you say your name is?"

My name is John Douglas Baker, but I go by Doug because my father's name is John, too.

"Mr. Baker here saved the day," Jewels explained to my boss when she and I returned to the restaurant that night. My boss, a well-known Chicago restaurateur named Fred Fleischman, laughed as Jewels told the story of our mad pursuit, but that was mostly because Jewels was doing the talking and my boss, like everyone, liked Jewels.

Later that night, after the restaurant closed, Fred pulled me aside and said, "If someone bolts, let him bolt. It's not worth the fuss. I thought you said you'd done this before. How old are you really?"

"Twenty-three," I lied. "Honest."

I was too scared to ask Fred about Jewels, but I would come to learn that she was a restaurant regular. She ate very little, drank a lot, smoked too much, told funny stories, left generous tips, listened to anybody's troubles, never met a stranger. You knew the nights when Jewels was going to show up: You could *feel* her coming.

Sometimes she arrived with friends, older women, widows like herself; but most often she came alone, asking for the corner booth in the bar so she could "dish the dirt with my *real* friends," the waiters, waitresses, bartenders and busboys—all of whom were half her age.

"You should get to know Jewels," one of the waitresses, Lilly, advised me early on. "She's really the best friend any of us have."

Jewels would become my best friend, too, but that took some time.

In those days, I was fiercely determined to make a go of my new life, on my own, without anyone's help—and within the narrowly defined parameters I had set for myself I had somehow come to believe that meant without friendship or family, as well. I always had been much of a loner and I now saw no reason to change.

Jewels thought otherwise. "Loners are losers," she told me the second or third time we met. "What in the world have you got to be so alone about?"

The dining room had closed for the night and our bartender had already announced last call. Jewels stood shoulder-to-shoulder with a pack of waiters and waitresses trying to convince me to join them at another bar down the street.

"Not tonight," I said.

"Lilly says you say that every night," Jewels replied. She had her baby blues fixed on me again.

"I've got to get back to my apartment," I said. My "apartment" was actually a room in an apartment Fred Fleischman rented for Lilly. Fred's wife apparently knew about the arrangement with Lilly—and didn't seem to mind. Fred didn't care that Lilly was making a little side money off of renting to me, as long as I kept my mouth shut about who came, went or stayed.

"Oh, you'll get back to *your* apartment," Jewels said, fully understanding the situation. Then she added, "eventually." She laughed at that and took a step forward. For Jewels, conversation was almost always conducted within a matter of inches. "Come on, Doug," she whispered. "It's just for one, maybe two, drinks."

"I don't think I should," I said.

Jewels started to argue, but stopped. Then she smiled and relaxed her slender shoulders. She wagged a finger at me and conceded, "You win. Tonight. But you should know something, darling. You don't get away from Jewels that easy."

She was right, of course.

One night, Jewels had dinner at the restaurant with her niece, a quiet, curly haired redhead who lived with her parents, Jewels' sister and brother-in-law, in Winnetka.

"Douglas, how old are you?" Jewels asked as she and her niece were putting on their coats to leave.

"Ah, twenty-three," I said. "Almost twenty-four."

"Nonsense. Besides, that's too old for my niece. How old are you really?"

"Eighteen," I said, "but that's a secret around here."

Jewels shook her head. "You should know that secrets are fine, but it's ridiculous to lie about your age. How would you like to take my niece to dinner sometime?"

The niece blushed as red as her hair, then laughed sharply, clutching Jewels' sleeve. I smiled as I felt my own throat warming with a blush.

"Yes or no, Douglas. Wendy's been carping about lack of love all night long and you're a perfectly respectable young man."

The niece rolled her eyes from behind the curls. "I'm so sorry," she said. "Sometimes my aunt can be—"

"No," I said sharply, my mouth dry, the word falling out like a scratched-off paint chip. "I mean, yes. I mean, sure, let's, sure. Why not?"

Wendy smiled.

"Yes," Jewels exclaimed. "Why in the world not?"

I smiled. "Dinner?" I asked.

Wendy and I stood looking at one another until Jewels drummed her fingers across the wooden reservation desk. "My-oh-my," Jewels groaned.

"At this rate, we'll be here all night. Say, 'Yes,' darling."

Wendy blushed even deeper. "Yes," she said.

"A triumph!" Jewels exclaimed.

That first date turned out to be a disaster—we had nothing in common, except for Jewels, and after an hour Wendy asked if we could speak about something other than her aunt. For a week-and-a-half after the date I successfully dodged Jewels, dreading the moment when I would have to come clean and say, "You're niece is nice, but dull."

Finally, Jewels cornered me in the restaurant lobby and, with my back literally up against the wall, I blurted out my confession: "The date had been"—now how had I put it?—"lackluster."

Jewels gave me one of her long looks again.

"I don't know," I started babbling. At that time, I always spoke rapidly when I spoke from the heart. "Maybe I shouldn't have said that. I don't know. I think maybe I shouldn't date. Maybe I shouldn't get mixed up in all of that."

Jewels shook her head. I braced myself for a burst of anger for in those early days I didn't really know Jewels and simply expected everyone I met to have a gunfire temper. Just a little something else given to me by my father, I suppose.

"Remember," I said. "You've got to remember. You pretty much forced the whole date on us."

Jewels shook her head again before finally letting her stare fall from my eyes. She sighed, lit a cigarette and shook her head once more. "Did Wendy really say she was tired of talking about me?"

I nodded.

Jewels lifted her eyes slowly. "In that case," she said, failing to hide her smile, "the little tramp is out of the will."

As we grew closer, Jewels began to push me—to date, to find a better job, to do this or that. One afternoon, Jewels and I walked along Michigan Avenue on our way to Water Tower. Spring was coming and Jewels had convinced me it was time to buy new clothes.

"You're far too skinny," she had said. "Maybe some big clothes will help."

She somehow made it sound like shopping was my idea and insisted on buying whatever I wanted. Afterward, as we waited on a crowded street corner for the traffic light to turn green, Jewels lit a cigarette and I suddenly felt uneasy about Jewels buying me a wardrobe.

"I'm really quite capable of purchasing my own clothes," I protested. She paid no attention. "I can make up my own mind. I can afford whatever I really need. I can—"

"Look," she said, pointing across the street with her hand holding the cigarette. "That man's in trouble."

I looked up just in time to see an obese man wearing a dark suit, white shirt and loosened tie grab his chest, stagger and collapse backward onto the sidewalk. Another bulging man wearing a dark suit lunged for his stricken friend, shouting: "Oh my God, oh my God."

With traffic still moving, Jewels elbowed through the pedestrians around us, leaped off the curb and hurried across the sunny intersection. I was right behind her, carrying three shopping bags. Horns honked. Drivers slammed on their brakes.

Once across the street, Jewels knelt beside the fallen stranger and shook his shoulders. "Darling! Darling! Can you hear me?"

The man didn't respond.

Jewels looked up at the worried face of a tall, wide-eyed woman. "Call an ambulance," Jewels ordered, then dipped her ear to the man's mouth. After a moment, she lifted her head and faced me. "Watch my loot," she said, thrust her purse into my hands, tossed her cigarette into the gutter, slipped off her mink and threw it at me. A crowd closed in around us.

Jewels leaned forward and blew two big breaths into the man's mouth. His chest rose slightly. Jewels tried feeling a pulse on the guy's rubbery neck and then his thick wrist. She tore open his shirt, folded her hands at the center of his white chest and began pumping.

"One one thousand, two one thousand, three one thousand, four one thousand . . ."

She stopped, blew two breaths into the man's mouth and resumed the chest thrusts.

"One one thousand, two one thousand, three one thousand, four one thousand, five one thousand, six one thousand—come on, darling, breathe . . ."

The tall, wide-eyed woman nudged through the tight crowd beside me and said: "I called them. I called them. They're coming."

Jewels blew into the stranger's mouth again.

"Oh my God," the man's friend was still shouting.

"One one thousand, two one thousand, three one thousand, four one thousand—come on, darling, breathe . . ."

I hadn't heard the sirens, but the paramedics appeared in no time and descended upon the man. Jewels rose slowly, looking tired and grim. I tried handing back her purse, but she let her hands hang motionless at her sides. For the first time, I noticed her hands looked knotted and old.

The wide-eyed woman whispered to Jewels, "Is he going to die?"

I draped the mink over Jewels' thin shoulders. She stared at the paramedics crouching over the man. Her eyes were flat.

"I've got a pulse," one paramedic finally said and Jewels clenched my arm, exhaling a breath she and all of us must've been holding for minutes. Within another few moments, the paramedics began lifting the man into the ambulance.

I handed Jewels her purse again. She reached inside, retrieved a pocket mirror and a lipstick. She had the lipstick at her lips when she noticed her cigarette in the gutter.

"Damn," she said. "My last Pall Mall."

The stranger's companion stepped forward and held a cigarette toward Jewels. "Maybe this will do," he offered. "Thanks for helping my friend. You're some broad."

Jewels smiled at that and snapped the pocket mirror shut. She blinked tears from her eyes and stretched on tiptoes to kiss the man's chubby cheek.

"That's sweet," she said. "But you don't have to thank me, darling. We're all in this together."

I have years of memories of Jewels, years of stories.

The New Year's Eve she rear-ended a squad car on Clark Street. She wiggled out of the ticket by making a date with the cop, who had gone to high school with her sister.

The time I was broke and broken, having just been fired by Fred Fleischman from the restaurant job—collateral damage after his affair with Lilly finally fizzled. I put what money I had saved into an apartment of my own and the very next day found myself undergoing emergency knee surgery. Before I could find another restaurant job, I was forced to hobble around on crutches for weeks. Fortunately, Jewels showed up at my door the next day carrying two armloads of the sort of groceries only Jewels would buy. For years, I kept the bamboo shoots.

I remember an autumn afternoon, too, when Jewels and I were walking past Buckingham Fountain and I asked her, "Why haven't you remarried?" Jewels merely hugged my arm, turned her face toward the gray wind, and kept us walking.

One other afternoon we went to a Lincoln Avenue pantomime performance that neither of us really wanted to see, and less than a minute into the show Jewels sang out to the costumed characters: "I . . . caaan't . . . heaarrrr . . . youuu!" It was a bad joke, a dumb joke, but it stirred some mischief and Jewels loved mischief.

Once, at a political fundraiser for a conservative Senate candidate who was a friend of a friend—but not that close of a friend—Jewels silenced our banquet table by announcing, "Well, of course, he *tells* everyone he's against abortion, but he's assured me privately that he's all for it."

I took her to task on another occasion for creating some now-forgotten controversy that at the time I didn't think was so funny. But she countered with a wink, a wave of her cigarette and a compelling retort: "Oh, loosen up, darling."

Sometime in our first year together, as Jewels and I became increasingly fond of each other, the nearly forty-year difference between our ages caused its own mischief and started talk behind our backs. Naturally, Jewels delighted in every rumor: that I was her nephew, that I was her lover, that I was her nephew *and* her lover. She never admitted such, but I am certain Jewels started several of the rumors herself because she always laughed the hardest when someone revealed the latest tidbit.

However, such rumors were discomforting for me, for many reasons no doubt, and for one reason in particular. One evening as Jewels and I were leaving the Music Box Theatre, I stood behind her, holding her cotton sweater in the battered lobby of the old movie house and—these moments always sound corny, I know—I realized I had fallen in love. Not love as I've come to know it now years later, and most certainly not love as I used to imagine it then when I was so intent to be alone.

This was another kind of love.

A new kind of love.

And I was scared.

"Men don't know nothing 'bout love," Jewels used to say. "Even Malloy. And Malloy was the shrewdest Irishman who ever lived."

Harry Malloy introduced himself to Jewels when she was twenty-two years old and had just moved with her sister to Chicago from a small town in eastern Pennsylvania, more precisely, from a small dairy farm owned and operated by her widowed father. ("Honestly, darling, tell me the truth," Jewels once confided, nudging her Caesar salad aside as she propped her thin elbows on a café table. "Can you picture *me* milking a cow?")

Harry Malloy was then twenty-seven, born and raised in Sligo, now living in Chicago. I never knew for sure—still don't—what Malloy did for a living. "He was just someone who owned things," Jewels once explained.

Jewels met Harry in The Emerald Club, a northside jazz joint, one of those many, old places now closed, a former Capone speakeasy with tall copper ceilings and green lights where most everyone drank gin. Jewels lived two blocks away with an older cousin and Malloy was boozing with four friends, celebrating someone's upcoming marriage.

"Malloy proposed to me that very night, about an hour after we met,"

Jewels recalled, tapping a shiny red thumbnail against her white teeth. "He must have been swept up in the romantic moment."

Jewels thanked him for the proposal, but nonetheless declined.

"How about dinner then?" Malloy asked. He was lanky, tall enough to tower over Jewels, and what she described as Bogart-handsome. "I'm really quite polite when I'm not around these fellas," he explained.

Harry Malloy was polite, it seems, and much more. He and Jewels had dinner, then dated again and again, until an evening three months later when they were back in the Emerald. This time, it was just the two of them, snuggled in a rounded booth.

"Let's get married," Malloy said again. "Right away."

Jewels laughed and pressed a finger to his lips and asked why in the world he was so anxious.

He kissed her finger and replied, "Because I love you."

Jewels rested her head against the broadness of Malloy's chest and sighed. "You don't really love me," she whispered. "Not yet. You've got yourself convinced you do, but you don't." She looked up at Malloy's square jaw and frowning face, and smiled. "You're just afraid of being alone," she told him. "But don't worry, darling. Eventually you will really love me."

They were married within the week.

Time passed, with happy days and sad days, days with friends and days without children. A year after their marriage, Jewels was diagnosed with cancer. "Just a small cancer," was how she described it to me.

Small, perhaps, but nonetheless brutal. The cancer was removed, but left her unable to bear children.

"Malloy was weeping," she recalled, "and I asked him not to cry because I so badly didn't want to think about how much I wanted a baby. But then he told me he was crying because he was so happy—he had thought the cancer was going to kill me and he was so relieved when the doctors told him I would live."

When Jewels told this story, as when she told most any story about Harry Malloy, she looked beyond me, beyond everything in the cluttered front room of her Lincoln Park townhouse, and smiled. A not-lonely, not-unhappy smile.

"You know what I said to Harry?" she recalled. "I told him, 'You're relieved? Imagine my surprise.'"

I laughed at that then and I can laugh at that now, but when I first heard her story I was young and couldn't help feeling sorrow beneath our laughter.

When Jewels and I stopped laughing, I shook my head and mumbled,

"We're born alone and we die alone."

Jewels looked straight toward me then, leveling one of her long looks. We were seated near tall windows, in the morning sunshine, in facing arm chairs. Her smile was gone.

"You should know something, darling," Jewels said, exhaling cigarette smoke between tight lips. "Your youth sometimes makes you say the most foolish things."

In time, I was always saying foolish things around Jewels because that's what happens when you take the risk of telling someone everything—and, with time, I told Jewels everything.

About day-to-day things, yes: work, who said this, who did that, guess who came into the restaurant last night. But about other things, too, more important things—family things. Things about my father, my mother and me, for instance.

"I've never really told you," I once explained to Jewels, "but my father hates me. And he's not really a hateful man."

We were driving in her Lincoln, some time in fall. We were heading north on Lake Shore Drive. Jewels was behind the wheel, leaning back deeply into the seat. I was staring out the passenger window, watching choppy waves.

"He hates me because I killed Mom," I said.

I had never before spoken these words and I was not fully aware why I was uttering them now. I felt my stomach tremble as I took a breath. "Mom had no problem when she was pregnant, but something awful happened at my birth. It killed her, but let me live."

Jewels reached for my hand from across the seat.

"My father always blamed me," I continued. I was still looking out the window and starting to cry. "And I guess I can't blame him."

Jewels squeezed my clammy hand. I couldn't stop the tears from coming.

"Darling," Jewels said, putting both hands on the steering wheel.

I twisted to face her. I was shaking, speaking fast. "Please don't tell me that it's not my fault," I snapped, "that, therefore, I shouldn't feel bad. I *know* it's not my fault. I know for damn sure, no matter *what* my father says, no matter what even I say, it's not my fault . . . But still—"

Jewels didn't look at me. "I wasn't going to say that, darling."

I wiped tears with the back of my hand. "Then please don't tell me not to be so harsh on my father." My stomach muscles tightened with rising anger.

Jewels kept her eyes on the road and started moving her car faster, weaving in and out of traffic. "I wasn't going to say that either, darling."

"Then please don't tell me to just calm down, to just put it all away in my past."

Jewels shook her head and bit her lower lip. We seemed to be moving too fast. She spoke: "What would you tell your mother if you could say anything to her now—right now—at this moment?"

"What?"

"What would you tell your mother if you could say anything to her right now?"

I gripped the seat. We were speeding. "I don't know," I said. "I'd tell her, 'I'm sorry.'"

Jewels didn't say a word.

"I'm sorry," I said again.

Jewels looked at me then, through her own eyes brimming with tears. She placed her warm hand over mine. We were flying.

"I forgive you," she said. "With all my heart, I forgive you."

Family secrets are the deepest secrets and for years I did not fully understand the meaning of what had really happened during those few minutes on that autumn day as Jewels and I sped along the lake shore, half fighting and half fighting back the tears. I, of course, had assumed it had only to do with me—with my father, my mother, my problems; problems I'm still and forever will be turning over. But it had to do with Jewels, as well.

As close as Jewels and I were, there was much we did not share, much we left unquestioned and unexplained. I recognize now I only learned about Jewels in bits and pieces, over time, with many loose ends. I suppose that's the way we learn about most people, but it seems particularly true of Jewels.

A loose end from her friend, Maggie: "I can't believe she hasn't ever told you about the time she danced in the Kennedy White House. The President—*Jack*, she called him *Jack!*—was a little drunk and kept stepping on her toes, but she didn't care. They did the samba. Get her to tell *that* story."

From her cousin, Anna: "Once when we were living together—God this was years and years and years ago—this little guy with a cut-up face showed up at my front door and asked for Jewels. Well, I told him to just go away, but then Jewels elbowed me aside, opened the screen door and ushered this fellow inside. They spoke Spanish or Mexican or something. I just about fell over. Then Jewels ran and got her handbag and pulled out a wad of cash and gave it all to the little guy. I just about croaked. I mean, really, I had absolutely no idea—no idea whatsoever—what was going on. Well, the guy thanked her and thanked her and turned to me and smiled and once he finally left I asked Jewels what *that* was all about and you know what Jewels said? Jewels said, 'What, darling? What was what all about?' as if *nothing* had just happened. And I said, 'That Mexican and that money.' And she just kind of shrugged. She said his name was Ramon and she knew him from the restaurant where he worked. He was going through some tough times, she said, and he needed just a bit of help. And then Jewels told me to mind my own business."

From her friend, Tammy: "Jewels was invited to all of the parties—everybody always loved Jewels. I dare you to find someone who didn't."

And from someone who didn't, her sister-in-law, Bea: "Hasn't Jewels told you how she killed Harry?"

Grief.
Anger.
Jealousy.

"Hasn't Jewels told you how she killed Harry?" I have now spoken with Harry Malloy's sister a countless number of times and throughout it all Bea has always worn the same three faces of pain.

I met Bea when Jewels and I were attending a fireworks party at someone's big summer home on Lake Geneva. The party had started with a noisy crowd on the green lawn in the hot afternoon and had ended with me by myself on the dock after it was late enough to be considered early. Jewels must have been up at the house and I was trying to sober up by staring at the sunrise on the water. Still heat rose from the lake and my mind remained cloudy from the hours of wine and champagne throughout the night before.

A heavy woman in pink, Bea, was all of a sudden standing over me.

"You're Jewels' young friend," she said.

At the time, I had no idea who Bea was, so I tried smiling.

"If I were you," she said, "I'd be careful. I'd be damned careful." Bea leaned down toward me. Her face—a red, jumbo face with empty, doughnut eyes and ample chins—quivered.

I was still a little drunk and still tried smiling.

"She killed her husband. Hasn't Jewels told you that? Hasn't Jewels told you how she killed Harry?"

Bea was right on top of me.

"Did she 'forget' to mention how she got drunk at that party and insisted on driving home? Hasn't Jewels explained how she lost control and smashed their car? How she walked away without so much as a scratch but how Harry was killed?"

I tried standing, but found myself weak under the heat and hangover. I had to look away from Bea. "Excuse me," I mumbled.

"Jewels killed Harry."

"Excuse me," I mumbled again. "I cannot speak with you. I have to go."
"You better be careful."

"I have to go," I said again, stood, stumbled, and started to hurry up the lawn toward the house.

"Run!" Bea shouted after me and I ran, convinced I was being chased by her sugary voice. "Run! But be careful. Be so damned very careful!"

Jewels found me a while later sitting in the cool shade on the house's front porch steps, rocking with my knees against my chest. "Douglas," Jewels said softly, letting her hand touch my shoulder and the back of my head.

She stepped down to stand before me and, finally, to look beyond me. She looked beyond everything and nodded. "I just spoke with Bea," she said. "I'm sorry I never told you before. I'm sorry I wasn't the one to tell you now."

I reached forward and held Jewels' hands. Looking back now, I realize I had learned from Jewels how to provide comfort, as well.

"Not a day goes by that I don't think about Malloy," she said. I stood and we hugged. I kissed her softly above her eyes, and listened.

"When Malloy died, I was a mess," Jewels explained slowly. "Thought I was losing my mind. Made the mistake of moving in with Bea, so she could look after me and my grief. That only made matters worse. Bea was always trouble, for me, for Malloy, for everyone—but after Malloy died, she became something mean."

Jewels embraced me again, squeezing me even tighter before holding me away so she could look into my eyes as she spoke. Her eyes appeared gray. "Came close to killing myself," she said. "One thing stopped me. I remembered a time from about two years before, when we received a telephone call late one night and Malloy had to rush out to resolve another one of Bea's trumped-up, so-called 'emergencies.' I told Malloy to stay, to let Bea handle whatever it was this time by herself. But Malloy said, 'No.' He gave me a quick kiss, on the cheek, and said, 'No . . . We're all in this together.'"

Jewels squeezed me tight again and sighed against my chest. "That's what kept me alive," she said. "And that's what keeps me going."

Years of memories, years of stories: the time Jewels taught me to jitterbug outdoors in Grant Park . . . the time she donated her Lincoln to an old folk's home, declaring, "From now on, I walk" . . . the time she learned the last, worst news—the news that she had once again been diagnosed with cancer.

It had started with a fall, a swift and crippling pain that took her legs away. There were no jokes this time, no light-hearted dismissals of "just a small cancer." Jewels had it bad and it hurt.

Doctors recommended treatments and friends recommended listening to doctors, but Jewels was adamant with me: "No treatment, darling. No knives. No radiation. No nothing. I'm ready."

At first, of course, I protested, trying to persuade her that she was still young . . .

"Age has nothing to do with it," she'd reply. "I'm ready."

. . . that she was giving up . . .

"I'm not giving up," she'd say. "I'm *ready*."

. . . that I didn't want her to die . . .

"Thank you."

But in the end, Jewels had it her way. She was determined to teach this last lesson, as well.

"Remember what your old boss, Fred Fleischman, once told you," Jewels said. "'If someone bolts, let him bolt. It's not worth the fuss.'"

I achieved only the most minor of victories: Jewels agreed to fill a prescription for pain medication and she agreed to my staying at her townhouse to help her look after things while greeting five weeks of afternoon visitors who each came to say good-bye.

Jewels remained cheery during those afternoon visits, but we spent the nights alone, almost always in silence, which was perhaps the first silence between us, as if we had been saving our silence for just when we would need it the most.

At night, the pain pills Jewels swallowed really doped her up and for a few minutes before she fell asleep, Jewels usually wound up in a sort of loopy state. She'd close her eyes, and bow her head, and repeat anything I said.

"Get some sleep now," I'd say. "Get some sleep," she'd say.

"I'll turn off the light," I'd say. "Turn off the light," she'd say.

But on this night, her last night, Jewels surprised me. She closed her eyes and turned her whitened face away. I pulled up the blanket across her chest.

"Get some sleep now," I said. "Get some sleep," she said.

"I'll turn off the light," I said. "Turn off the light," she said.

"I love you," I said, rose and turned to switch off the lamp.

"Yes," she whispered. "Did you ever think we could love each other so much?"

I stopped, looked over my shoulder. I wanted to ask Jewels to repeat what she had said because I was fearful I might forget those wonderful words. But Jewels was already asleep. And in the morning, she would not waken.

So I remember.

At times like this—when our youngest daughter gets wet-eyed, tight-faced angry and sobs, "Nobody loves me, nobody loves me"—I listen to my wife and I remember. I remember what it's like to feel alone in this world and I remember Jewels and, in time, I once again find my patience.

I face my redheaded wife. I squeeze Wendy's hand and she smiles and I smile, too, and, together, we climb the stairs, step by step, arm in arm, ready to comfort the tears and fears of our baby girl.

The Boys

*This is Frank Sinatra singing. Not Old Sinatra, with the barrel body,
the hollow voice. And not Young Sinatra, either: the too-skinny kid
with the too-wise grin leaning into a big floor mic in a black-and-white
glossy. This is Sinatra In His Prime. When he was cool and tough
and wore that hat on his album covers. When he was The Man.*

The Man sings of trouble and moonlight and love and romance.

You're happy to be here.

You're happy to be behind the wheel of the Mazda, heading out of
Chicago, rolling north up the interstate toward Lake Geneva.

You don't mind that it's about ten-thirty on a Saturday morning—
lately, you're not awake by then, even if you're not home—and you don't
mind that the sky is spring-gray and it's still cold enough to see your
white breath outside.

You don't mind because you're flying, you're doing 70 miles per hour,
and you're crunched in the car with the boys—O'Malley, O'Rilley and
Fitz—and you've got a big day, a great day, one hell of a day before you.

You're on a journey, you and your friends. You'll shoot some trap, win
some money at the dog races, and spend what's left of the night drinking
bottle after bottle of beer. And you'll talk about politics and music and
women—and men. For when men are among men all they ever really
talk about is men.

Right now, tearing along, you're speaking with O'Malley but half-listening to the Sinatra disc and half-listening to O.R. and Fitz in the back seat, as well.

O'Malley is talking about his bad date last month, up at the dog track, up at Dairyland in Kenosha. O'Reilly and Fitz are talking about work.

Actually, O'Malley's first date—the date at the races—had been fun. A setup. A friend and his wife had introduced O'Malley to one of his wife's co-workers, an accountant. The four of them had made an afternoon of it, lunch and betting on the dogs. O'Malley and the accountant had hit it off, O'Malley thought.

It was the second date that went bad: The date when O'Malley arrived at the accountant's house and she asked if he would mind if her girlfriend came along, too.

"Ouch," you say.

"Yeah, but," O'Malley says, "the races were fun. A great time. Today will be great fun, too."

"Great fun," you say, leaning back a little to better hear O.R. and Fitz. You used to work with O'Reilly and Fitzgibbons up until only a month ago, so their gossip is still fresh and of interest. "What are you guys talking about?"

"Bev," they moan and, together, their voices sound like locusts humming: "*Bevvvvvvvvvvvv.*"

You laugh and Fitz says: "Sure, easy for you to laugh. Mr. No-Longer-Work-There. Mr. Quit-Your-Job-To-Write. Mr. No-More-Have-To-Put-Up-With-Bev."

"The other day," O'Reilly says, "she screeched one of her screeches and I jumped out of my chair. Honest. I jumped out of my chair, right out of my desk. I can't work with that."

Fitz says: "Oh yeah!"

"I can't work with that," O'Reilly says again. "I've worked newsrooms. I've worked production sets. I've worked in noisy places, you know, under deadline—but she's, she's—"

Fitz says: "Oh yeah!"

"She's awful," O'Reilly says. He's laughing, but groaning at the same time. You're remembering Bev's jackal-cackle bouncing off the walls. "I. Can't. Take. It," O.R. says finally.

O'Malley looks at you like a big brother looks at his little brother. You've known O'Malley for about three hundred years and, though he's never met Bev, he's heard you tell more than your fair share of war stories about her.

O'Malley smiles. "You should have fired her before you left," O'Malley says—and O'Reilly and Fitz instantly agree.

"Well," you say. "I guess," you say. You know they're right. They're your friends, your good friends, you're among your very best friends—and they are *always* right. "You're right," you say.

"OF–COURSE–WE'RE–RIGHT!" Fitz barks and you all laugh, hard. Fitz has a way of making you laugh like that, from the gut. It's not just what he says, though often what he says is funny all by itself. But with Fitz you get the whole package: the big, smooshy face with the altar-boy innocent eyes and the devil-grin that just advertises "I'm Up To Something!" The voice, too: Fitz grew up in the suburbs, Bellwood and Elmhurst mostly, but his voice is all Chicago, full of *'demz* and *'doz* and *gots* where the *haves* should be. Plus, with Fitz, you get the acting and the actor's timing. He knows how and when to be funny.

O'Reilly starts singing along with Sinatra:

> "—*annddd, do you love me?*
> *Just like I love yooouuu—*"

Of the four of you, O'Reilly is the only one with any kind of singing voice, a baritone today made sandpaper rough by a cold.

He stops singing when he mentions Deborah. He's shaking his head.

Deborah is from the old job, too, a tall blonde, and you kind-of, sort-of have been dating her, though when anybody asks you always say, "We'll, we're just friends"—and you're certain that's Deborah's reply, too.

"She wanted to come today," O.R. says. He makes like the idea of Deborah—or any woman—joining the boys today would be the ultimate insult. You know: the old No-Girls-Allowed clubhouse rule.

"I told her no," you explain. "I told her this was just the boys. Guns, dogs—and the boys."

You recall how Deborah smiled and nodded and said: "Oh. A male bonding thing." And how you had said: "No. No, it's not like *that*."

You now look in the rearview mirror and see O'Reilly nodding but not smiling, like he's maybe really pissed. O.R. is the youngest of seven kids (interesting: you're all the youngest in your families) and being the youngest in a big family is a mixed blessing. Your parents have worked out most of the bugs in their parenting routine by the time you come along, but you also don't get your picture taken too often. By the time someone like a seventh kid comes along, everyone's grown rather weary of posing for family photographs.

But looking in the rearview mirror, you don't think O'Reilly is really pissed. He's gazing out the window and it occurs to you how his narrow face—with his short, curly, red hair and narrow chin, narrow nose—looks so serious when he's not smiling. Maybe this just occurs to you now because you're so accustomed to seeing O.R. smile so often.

Outside, farm fields and junkyards zip past on both sides of the road.

"I saw this PBS show the other night on the Kennedys," O'Reilly eventually says.

"*Bah-be,*" Fitz says, doing his best Boston-JFK-rip-off that's only funny because it's so bad. "*Hah bat sum chaw-dah?*"

Then the boys start talking politics, which pretty much means Democratic politics, and, like every conversation that occurs among Democrats, especially Irish-American Democrats, the talk, in no time at all, turns back to JFK and Bobby and Teddy . . . and the affairs . . . and the deaths . . . and, naturally, the movies.

"I watched 'Hoffa.'"

"Great movie."

"Nicholson is the best."

"You know the guy who plays Bobby Kennedy—when Kennedy goes after Hoffa? O'Malley went to grade school with that guy."

O'Malley nods.

"Really?"

"Kevin Anderson," O'Malley explains. "I remember he was always a nice kid—and fast. He could run really fast, in gym class, you know."

You look at O'Malley and think how, straight on, he sort of looks like Bobby Kennedy. But, in profile, he more resembles Abraham Lincoln. At any rate, he ultimately looks like, "White, Working Class Guy from Waukegan." You're all from white, working class families and towns pretty much like Waukegan.

You then tell everyone that Kevin Anderson may have been a nice kid, but, in your limited opinion, the Kennedys weren't always such nice boys.

"No," agrees O'Malley. "They were in politics. They had to be shrewd, pernicious."

There's a pause.

"Pernicious," you say.

"Oh," Fitz pipes in. "'Pernicious!'"

"Pernicious?" you say. "What's 'pernicious' mean?"

O'Malley starts to talk but the words fender-bender in his mouth. That doesn't usually happen to O'Malley. "Pernicious," he finally says. "It means . . . well," then you see him smiling. "It means shrewd."

"Oh!" Fitz says.

"Oh!" O'Reilly says.

And you, you say, "Oh!" too, just for the effect. "Pernicious."

You're all laughing again when you make the turnoff at Route 50. You're about 30 minutes now from where you want to be—the Americana Club, which used to be the old Playboy Club, years ago. Things change, as someone somewhere once said.

Now the Americana Club is a family resort with golf and tennis and a small ski hill and—what you've come for, why you and the boys are up and out on a Saturday morning: a shooting range.

You've come to press shotguns into your shoulders and raise your barrels and shoot your 350-pellet shells up into the gloomy sky at clay pigeons.

You've come to blast the hell out of some "trap."

You've driven all this way to "do some damage" and—yes, of course, what else?—to talk, to have fun, to be men among men.

Sinatra, again. Snapping his fingers. Tapping his foot. Smiling, slyly.
The Man sings of teardrops.

In Congress.

On cable.

Even at the big dinner table on family holidays.

You've heard a lot of talk about so-called "men's rights"—how men need to band together to *fight* for their rights, just as women, blacks and gays are doing. You've also heard a lot of jabbering about so-called "White Male Victimization"—how white men in particular are becoming increasingly shut-out as society takes baby steps toward the horizon of equality.

At some point during each of these conversations, someone—always a man, usually a white man—makes the statement that it's confusing and troubling to be a man in today's world.

That usually makes you laugh.

That usually makes you laugh and laugh.

That usually makes you laugh so hard it hurts.

And you're laughing now not because of such bellyaching; rather, it's the sight you see that's silly.

You're outside and the cold, soft wind is turning your faces red. Here you are, the boys and you, armed to the teeth, soldiers with not much to fight for, hunters with no real game.

Yet, you each juggle a semi-automatic Remington 1100 shotgun as you each dump a heavy box of 25 red-cased, 8-point, 12-gauge shells into your big coat pockets.

A guy named Lumpy smiles as he lines you up on the range semi-circle—you . . . then Fitz . . . then O'Reilly . . . and then O'Malley, each standing about three paces apart, facing west toward the winter remains of a gray and white cornfield.

Lumpy has worked for the Americana Club for some time so he's dressed to work outside: big boots, big gloves, big coat, and a hat and scarf, which only lets you see thin eyes behind smudged, windshield-sized goggles. Lumpy is one the range "pullers," which means he'll release your traps and give you tips on shooting better.

About 16 feet between you and the cornfield is a bunker-like concrete box. Lumpy holds the remote control, which will launch the orange trap from the cement bunker, flinging it upward into the sky—toward the left, toward the right, or straight ahead.

You're asked to shoot first.

You load the shell and manage to get the tip of your gloved finger caught when the "action"—the loading chamber for the shotgun shell—automatically closes. After you tug your glove away, you raise the shotgun, press it into your shoulder, lean forward, and take a breath.

"Pull," you say.

FWOOOOP: The orange trap rises, spinning like a tossed saucer to your left.

You raise your shotgun less than an inch and squeeze the trigger.

BOOOOOM: The trap explodes into one hundred pieces and you're smiling.

The boys are smiling, too.

"Oh, sure!" Fitz says. "Now I know why *you* wanted to do this."

The four of you start taking turns.

Fitz misses. O'Reilly misses. O'Malley misses. And you hit again. "Just lucky," you say and that's the truth.

Then Fitz hits one, and O.R. and O'Malley miss again.

When it's your turn once more, you grunt "pull" and squeeze the trigger. You can't miss if you tried. Fitz is low on his next shot and just before O.R. calls "pull," you say, "Think of Bev."

He blasts the hell out of it and you all laugh.

"*Bevvvvvvvvvvvvv*," O.R. sings, lowering his gun, all smiles.

You all laugh even harder when Fitz imitates Bev's jackal-cackle. And you keep on like that for a few more rounds, laughing and firing these big guns.

After a while you've all hit except O'Malley. In fact, up until this point, O'Malley has been flat lousy: the trap flies left and O'Malley shoots right; the trap flies right and there's O'Malley blasting away at nothing to the left.

When he misses yet again, you catch yourself making a face, then catch Fitz smiling at you.

"Hey," Fitz whispers, "did O'Malley take the big bus or the little bus to school?"

O'Reilly doesn't whisper his joke. "Guess we'll never have to worry about O'Malley assassinating some president," O'Reilly says.

And you all laugh again, including O'Malley. But you can tell O'Malley is really trying and truly disappointed.

"None of us has ever done this before," you tell him. Now it's your turn to play big brother, to comfort and to encourage. "You'll get it. It's just luck," you say. "Dumb luck."

And that's what you say again at the end of 25 rounds after you've come out on top. "It's just luck," you say and O'Malley nods, with his mouth closed tightly. "Dumb luck, that's all."

An hour later, you find you're repeating yourself once more.

"Just . . . dumb . . . luck," you're saying.

You've moved on to Dairyland Greyhound Park in Kenosha. There's evidence of change here, too. These days, you've noticed, almost all courses—for dogs, for ponies—look, feel and smell more like shopping malls than down-and-dirty racetracks. They have grandstands and club-houses, but "sports lounges," too. They have information booths where well-groomed women (not cigar-chomping old-timers) offer pleasant instructions regarding where you will find the betting windows. And Dairyland, in particular, feels compelled to note:

> Proper attire is required during all evening perfor-
> mances. No T-shirts, cut-off or gym shorts, or torn
> or faded jeans on the 2ND and 3RD floors of the
> facility. Bare feet will not be allowed.

At this point, bare feet are not your problem. Bare feelings are.

You're shoving a big handful of money—winnings!—into your pocket. Your first bet (a $6 boxed trifecta on the 1, 5 and 6 dogs in the 5TH race) paid $84.60.

"Just luck," you say.

"Jesus," O'Reilly says. "You *are* lucky."

O'Malley is still tight lipped but he does mumble, "Congratulations."

O'Malley isn't even betting. Maybe it's because, after the trap shoot-ing, he thinks he's on a roll of bad luck. Or maybe it's the memory of his bad date—and her girlfriend. Or maybe—

"I don't really know how this works," is how O'Malley explains his non-participation. "So I'm not going to do it. But you, well, you guys go right ahead."

The thing is: You don't know how it works, either—in fact, before placing the bet on your big win you had to ask Fitz what "boxed trifecta" meant . . . a fact, you notice, which isn't sitting so easy with Fitzgibbons. He had placed the same boxed trifecta bet, where you choose the top three dogs to finish in any order, but Fitz had picked the 4 dog instead of the 5 dog. You won. He lost. And Happy Fitzgibbons is most certainly not happy.

"I'll buy lunch!" you declare, deciding it's too early for the boys' mood to dip.

But Fitz and O'Reilly say, "No, you don't have to buy lunch," and O'Malley just says he's not hungry.

So you shrug and—except for O'Malley—the boys continue betting. And, in a way, your luck holds out toward evening: You don't win big again.

Fitz loses $31.80.

O'Reilly drops about $20.

O'Malley, of course, hasn't risked a dime.

For your part, you blow through all but 20 bucks of your initial winnings and, at the finish of the 13TH race, you announce in grand fashion: "Okay, okay. I'm buying the first round at Grant's!"

"Yes!" Fitz exclaims.

"Yes!" O'Reilly exclaims.

They're nodding—and fake smiling.

"Yes!" they say. "That you are!"

You laugh again, but notice that O'Malley doesn't say a word.

Sinatra. He's grinning now. He knows something you don't.
The Man sings of fiddlers—and of facing the music.

You suppose it *is* confusing and troubling to be a man in today's world but you've still got to laugh.

"Ah, the good ol' days," so many people—men, mostly, usually white men—seem to be saying.

"The good ol' days," they say, never really pinpointing when those good ol' days were, though the suggestion always conjures for you a picture of the Kennedy boys or of Frank Sinatra singing. Frank Sinatra, in his prime.

"The good ol' days," so many say, "when men were *Men.*"

That's often followed with "and women were *Women.*"

And it frequently implies "when men were other White, Heterosexual, English-speaking, Middle-class Guys with Wives and Families and Mortgages and Lawns to Mow—just . . . like . . . me!"

You suppose these days are confusing and troubling and worrisome and all that, but you've still got to laugh because you feel like telling these men: "Hey, fellas: Get ready for change. The Just-Like-Me days? They're over."

For O'Malley, this night's over. He assures you he's just tired and simply doesn't feel like drinking; he asks you to drop him off at home on your way back downtown. You do and as O'Malley lumbers out of the car, the three of you invite him once more to join you but he declines, reassuring you he's just tired, just tired, after all. He gives you a smile.

So you say good-bye to O'Malley and head down to Grant's Tavern.

These past few months you've hit a lot of bars, your friends and you: Grant's MaGee's Ten Cat Cody's Glasscott's Andy's Lucky's Shelter High Tops The Green Mill Oz The Black Cat El Jardin Smart Bar 950 Southport City Saloon Hitchcock's The Lodge Hang-Ups The Store. The bars all run together and are pretty much the same: People come to drink and have fun; only the music changes.

Perhaps the music is changing, too, you think, for the American man. Perhaps the dance is different, the steps more complicated to master. But the funny thing is: The music must change, the dance must grow more complex. That is the consequence of progress, the Nature of All Life. And despite a few grumbles to the contrary, the cold fact remains that men are still in control, that life has not changed that much . . . yet. Men may see trouble ahead but, tonight, the moonlight is no less bright.

And tonight, as you have done on so many other occasions, you will press shoulder-to-shoulder as the night grows later and the bar becomes more crowded with more and more strangers. And you'll order beer after beer, and you'll speak louder until you lose your voice or lose your clarity of vision or lose your sense of balance. And you'll talk and laugh and slap one another on the back and enjoy being men among men, talking about politics and music and women—and luck.

Luck, you will note, has a way of moving around.

You'll talk about all that tonight, even though, at this moment, Fitz has grown rather quiet, adrift in a sea of private contemplations.

Hoping for a smile (the way one man reassures another that All is Well), you and O'Reilly tease Fitz that now *he's* being pernicious.

He smiles, vaguely, but doesn't fully re-ignite until the others—the women—begin to arrive. You had invited them to meet you at Grant's.

Connie shows first. She says you made a mistake by not inviting her to shoot. She grew up with guns and her father, as it turns out, is an expert shot, a lifelong clay shooter who came this-close to competing in the Olympics. Soon, Lisa joins you, as well. Lisa doesn't seem at all interested in your day's activities. Her husband is out with other pals and Lisa is just happy to have some time for herself.

Julie joins you, too. Julie doesn't let anybody get away with anything and she cocks an eyebrow when O.R. starts demonstrating for Julie's boyfriend how you stand when you shoot, how you keep your chin pressed to the stock, how you lift the barrel just a touch and then— *POW*—squeeze the trigger.

And Deborah joins you, at last. She's full of blonde smiles and strides to your table, saying hello, asking cheerily, "So how was this male bonding thing?"

"Great," you all say, you and Fitz and O'Reilly. You nod toward one another and, somewhere, think you hear a jackal-cackle. "It's been great," you all say. "Just great."

How Do You Like Me Now?

The sweaty German sitting next to me is blabbing on and on about how he'll never be afraid of anything anymore—nothing, not even torna-does, earthquakes and especially not plane wrecks—all because he lived through the bombing of Berlin as a child and no fear, no horror can compare with that.

I don't say a word.

I'm thinking of Dean.

The last time I saw Dean we had a fight, a serious fight, the kind of fight that usually ends relationships; but here I am an hour away from landing at O'Hare, thinking about Dean, hoping he'll meet me, wonder-ing if we can still make a go of it somehow, some way.

The German pokes our flight attendant and orders us both another round of drinks.

"Gin with tonic?" The flight attendant looks at me without smiling. She's a short-haired brunette and thin and pretty, of course.

"No tonic," I say. "I'll take it straight."

She walks away and the chubby German chortles, leans closer. "I like a man who drinks," he says. His thinning black hair is plastered to his rounded head. "I like a man who takes it straight."

The truth is I don't drink.

The truth is I go out of my way to avoid taking anything straight, I do just about anything to dodge reality, I hate facing facts.

I've just spent the past weekend in New Orleans at an academic conference where I presented a paper titled, "Paradox and Contradiction in Friedrich Nietzsche's 'The Gay Science.'" My paper was filled with facts, from margin to margin, page after page. But in real life—life away from thick books and crowded classrooms and heated conversations about theory—I am reluctant to confront facts.

And the fact is Dean doesn't love me anymore.

He told me so. He used those exact words. "David," he said early one morning, removing his square eyeglasses while sitting on the edge of our bed. He was dressed to play squash. "I don't love you anymore."

That's what we fought about this last time.

But I hate facing facts, and I don't want to be alone. I cannot live alone. I need Dean and he knows it.

"David," he told me once, with a sweet smile, in better days. "You need me."

I need someone. Something.

"People have irrational fears," the German says. His blue eyes twinkle. "Do you know what the chances are that you'll get hit by a tornado or crushed in an earthquake? Do you know how very slim the odds are that an airplane will crash—that this very airplane, this Flight 435, will fall from the sky right now as we're sitting here talking? Let me tell you something, my friend: The odds are in our favor *against* this happening. To fear otherwise is irrational and foolish."

Call me irrational.

I asked Dean why he doesn't love me anymore.

Call me foolish.

I asked if there was another man.

He said no.

I asked if I was pushing too hard for commitment.

He said no.

I asked if it was something I said or something I did.

He said no.

I asked why, then, why?

"Because I don't like you," Dean told me.

The flight attendant brings our drinks. She's still not smiling and I can't blame her.

"Here's to knowing no fear," the German says and touches his plastic cocktail cup to mine.

I can't help thinking it: What kind of reason is "because I don't like you"? After two years you don't just stop *liking* another person. And I still *like* him.

"Fourteen hours," the German says. "One bombing lasted fourteen hours. I remember crouching in the cellar, my sister beside me. Mother told us to cover our ears and close our eyes. But I was scared, so I looked and I listened. I remember the faces of the other mothers and children as the American bombers kept flying over and flying over—and their bombs kept falling and exploding, nonstop for fourteen hours. I tried hugging my mother, but she was scared, too. It never stopped: the bombers, their bombs. I tried hugging my sister, but she was more frightened than me. We prayed for it to stop. And, after a while, we thought it's just got to stop. But it didn't stop: The bombers kept coming, their bombs kept falling. For fourteen hours."

The German stares at his knees, which are tucked uncomfortably against the seat in front of him.

"It seemed like forever," he mumbles. He has the whitest skin.

I picture Dean greeting me in the airport terminal, smiling, opening his arms, asking about my success at the conference. In my imagination, Dean even repeats his joke—a lame joke that has sharpened into a bit of a taunt in the weeks leading up to New Orleans. "Did anyone ask, what's so gay about 'The Gay Science'?" And in my imagination, I see myself shaking my head at Dean's naughty remark and hugging Dean but thinking, *Yes, God is dead—and so am I.*

I wonder if Dean knows fear.

"Nothing bothers me now," the German says suddenly. "I have this perspective on life: If I can survive fourteen hours during a Berlin air raid, I can survive anything. There is nothing to fear. I can survive anything, everything."

I look at the German and he seems startled as I lean close.

"But can you survive love?" I ask.

When I speak, I realize I am drunk, slurring-my-words drunk, and it occurs to me those are the first words I have spoken to the German throughout our entire flight. My face inches closer still.

"Fourteen hours," he replies.

Some men, some really plain-looking men, actually appear more attractive the closer you get. Up close, this close, this obese and pasty German looks beautiful.

I ask if he likes me.

"Fourteen hours," he says again. "Mother went crazy with the waiting. She was a strong woman. But fourteen hours—she went out of her head. It killed my sister, too. In fact, only I endured."

I once again demand to know whether the German likes me. Our faces are a breath apart.

"Do you know how long fourteen hours can be?" he says.

I am the very last passenger to depart the airplane. I have said good-bye, good luck to my German seatmate. I have thanked the tired flight attendant who brought us our drinks and she has smiled, at last, in return.

I see Dean waiting, waiting for me, and he seems genuinely thrilled as I finally appear from an escalator into the crowded luggage claim area. He grins. He waves.

I walk straight toward Dean and think, *Yes, I love you, God, how I have missed you.* When Dean opens his arms to embrace me, I slap his face. Hard. His initial surprise instantly fires to red anger, but before Dean says a word I have the last word, I have the final say.

"How do you like me now?" I say.

He stands there, just stands there, with his mouth agape, rubbing his cheek.

I turn and walk away. My hand stings because I hit him so hard. I blow air onto my palm, small puffs of breath—and walk faster.

It's time to claim my baggage.

Punch Drunks

The day: The day ends in the big gym at St. Andrews Church, crowded behind, cramped behind, five white, middle-aged guys watching boxing. Golden Gloves boxing.

The guys: The guys all look the same, with the same rounded eye-glasses, the same rounded bodies, the same brownish-reddish crew-neck sweaters, too. And scattered beneath their folding chairs, littered beneath the black metal chairs, are tossed-aside beer cups, flattened popcorn boxes and waxy hotdog wrappers.

—*Put him down, Red*, one big guy growls toward the ring, eyes focused, face flushed. Big Guy stands. *Put him down!*

In the ring: In the ring, two Latino kids are fighting. Blue-shorts kid pummels red-shorts kid bad.

—*Get in tight*, Big Guy roars, mouth hanging open. *You gotta get in tight!*

Big Guy's friends: Big Guy's friends, they're shouting, too, a word here and there about this or that punch, a curse or two about the referee.

—*One punch, Red*, Big Guy hollers, meaty hands shaking. *One punch!*

The five guys: The five guys are all big guys and they all stop shouting, stop talking, when the standing Big Guy stretches and asks who needs a beer? One-by-one the round heads nod and these big guys say, these big guys say as one, *Yeah-me-I-do-sure-get-five.*

Then the standing Big Guy looks back toward the ring and groans, groans like a wounded buffalo. *What the fu . . . ?*

Blue-shorts: Blue-shorts' gloved fists, high above his head, making an X-shaped cross, marking victory. Red-shorts is standing, but standing empty, like an old beer cup, crushed, sweaty and tired.

Big Guy moans again, *What the fu . . . ?* Then maybe he remembers the church, maybe he remembers St. Andrew Himself and the X-shaped cross or maybe he remembers there's another beer coming, another fight, too.

—*Who's next?* Big Guy says, looking away from the ring toward his friends. *Whoever, whatever, I'm betting on Red.*

Patsy

So Bug O'Connor and Vivian Wynn stop for gas at a small one-pump-and-grill roadhouse in the middle of Kentucky. Bug wants a drink, needs gas, but he and Vivian, they're broke: They've been living the high life all the way since New York City—too much good food, too many expensive hotels, and, especially for this Vivian, way too much gin. Vivian: A few miles back, she finished the gin and passed out. Now, she sits in the convertible's front seat with her red head on her sunburned arm on the passenger door.

Bug looks at her, wipes sweat from his flat forehead with the palm of his hand. He gets to thinking about leaving Vivian. He reaches into the pocket of his black-and-white checkered sports jacket, folded on the wide seat between them. He removes a silver cigarette case, a love gift Vivian spent too much money on before they left Manhattan. With his thumb nail, he snaps open the case. It's empty.

Bug has just spent the better part of 1958 in jail—some two-bit scam, as usual. In jail, his cell mate, Elmore: He asked Bug to look up his girl. That got Bug to thinking, too. And Bug eventually found the girl—an orange-lipped chorus girl, this Vivian—and he sweet-talked his way into her heart and behind the wheel of her Buick. All this Vivian saw was slick-haired Bug and starlight. They were in love, they both said. They would never look back, they both said. They would begin a new life together in New Orleans.

Now Bug O'Connor thinks about getting up, just stepping out of the car, walking away. He thinks how dreams never turn out quite the way they seem at first. He considers just marching up and over that next hill, just leaving this lump of Vivian right there in the noontime sun to wake up and sober up and go home, alone.

But the big-eyed kid who pumps the gas: He's all of a sudden, out of nowhere, standing at Bug's door.

"I love Buicks," the kid says. He's tall, with a big nose and a large mouth. Bug thinks he looks like a fish. "Fill it up?" the kid asks.

"Fill it up," Bug croaks. "Hot day."

The kid: He moves around to the rear of the car, and Bug: He once again gets to thinking. He figures that when the kid gets this close to topping off the gas tank, he'll ask the kid for a pack of smokes and when the kid lumbers inside, Bug will just tool away, without paying. Bug drums the steering wheel with his chubby fingertips. He glances at Viv, who hasn't moved as much as a mummy. Bug looks back over his shoulder at the kid.

"Come here, son," he says, and the kid: He's a good kid, he does as he's told. "Can I ask you a favor?" Bug says. He shows the kid the empty cigarette case. "Can I ask you to run inside and get me a pack of Camels—just add it to the gas."

The kid looks straight at Bug. The sun reflects off the case, right into the kid's eyes.

"I love Patsy Cline," the kid says.

Bug's eyes get big. "How's that?"

"I love Patsy Cline," the kid repeats. "That's her singin'."

Bug shifts his body toward the roadhouse and listens. It's an old wooden, once-painted-red roadhouse, with a low, wide, black roof and screened-in windows. There's a gravel parking lot, no other cars. A Patsy Cline record is playing, on the jukebox, inside.

"And smell that ham," the kid says. There's a warm breeze. "Mama's cookin' a big ham for lunch today."

Bug hears the music—something or other about a weeping willow—and smells the ham. The aroma: It takes Bug back to the small kitchen of his grandmother's home in Albany—and Bug: He gets to thinking once more.

He turns back toward the kid, clears his throat, leans forward. He lowers his voice, raises his eyebrows, blinks some stinging sweat from his eyes. "Can you," he asks the kid. "Can you keep a secret?"

The kid: He nods, all earnest-like. Few secrets are ever revealed at this dusty roadhouse.

"Now you have to promise—cross your heart, kiss your hand to God—not to tell a soul," Bug says and the kid nods again.

Bug thumbs at Vivian over his shoulder. She's still dead asleep. "This," Bug says. "This is Miss Patsy Cline."

The boy's mouth: It falls open. He's got yellow teeth and Bug actually jerks back a little, frightened he might get bit.

"You're lyin' to me, mister," the kid says, but Bug: He catches the tone in the kid's voice, he's certain this kid *really* wants to believe.

"Why would I lie?" Bug says, pitching the kid a fast grin. "Miss Cline is sleeping. She had a big show last night. We're on our way to another show tonight. I manage her."

The kid stretches on tiptoes to look over the top of Bug's head, to get a better look at Vivian, whose face is getting redder under the sun.

"Miss Patsy Cline," the kid gasps.

The kid works here, Bug thinks. The kid works here, nowhere, and he's just old enough to begin wanting, to start feeling that life owes him more. The kid, Bug thinks, is convinced. The gag: It's hatched.

Bug snaps the cigarette case closed and slips it back into his jacket pocket. From there, Bug does most of the talking. The kid's eyes: They stay fixed on Vivian.

"Does your Mama like Patsy Cline songs?" Bug says. "Well, isn't that swell. How about your Daddy? No—just up and left? Well, every boy should have his mother to look after him. And your Mama must be a wonderful cook, that ham smells mighty fine. Stay and eat? I don't think we have the time . . . but I suppose we *could* make the time. I am a bit on the hungry side, now that you mention it. Why don't you just unhook that gas hose—we'll square up later—and I'll just park us around in the shade. Okay, you go ahead and tell your Mama we're coming in. Yes. Yes. Well, of course you can tell her. She's about to shake hands with the famous Patsy Cline."

The kid: He kicks up dust running on his big legs back into the road-house. He lets the squeaky screen door slam shut against the wooden frame behind him. Bug: He pulls the car to the cooler side of the road-house and begins shaking Vivian's round shoulders.

"Pretend you're Patsy Cline," he's saying. "You've got to pretend you're Patsy Cline. We're gonna hit up this kid and his mother for some gas and some food."

Vivian's eyes: They're stuck shut. Bug: He's shaking Vivian hard enough to shake loose her hair.

"And some gin," Vivian finally mumbles.

"Yes," Bug says. "And some gin—*if* you play this right."

Bug finally shakes Vivian hard enough to open her eyes. "Just remember," he says, "you're Patsy Cline."

Vivian blinks and smiles. She lifts one hand above her eyes to break the brightness of the day. She lifts the other to pull a hair from her mouth.

"Who's Patsy Cline?" she says.

"A singer," Bug snaps. His eyes are white and wide.

"Really?" Vivian's smile widens. "I'm a singer, too, you know."

Bug stops and looks straight at Vivian, right into her eyes. He smiles, sweetly, adoringly.

"You're an angel," he says. "How'd I ever get so lucky?"

Inside the roadhouse, all afternoon: The kid and his fidgety mother are as hospitable as can be. They pull out painted-white chairs for their visitors, they tug closed hand-sewn curtains to block out the sun. They rush to pour drinks, then rush to refill them. They sit on the edges of their seats and listen to Bug talk and talk and talk. Mostly, though, they just stare at Vivian—who, more than once, feels obliged to apologize for "the mess my hair must be in."

When the ham is ready, both the boy and his Mama bustle back into the kitchen to fix the plates. Bug: He overhears the murmur of their excited whispering and he turns to Vivian, barely able to contain himself.

"We've got 'em," he says, grinning as wide as a dinner plate. "We've got 'em good."

The meal is as tasty as it gets—tender, hot ham, potatoes mashed and puddled with gravy, fresh green peas spooned on the side, and warm biscuits nestled in a basket.

Mama, all nervous about this impromptu gathering, paws her napkin, quite unsure whether to leave the small, blue cloth nestled in her lap or clutched in her hand. Mama just about holds her breath until Vivian says, with genuine appreciation, "This is delicious, baby. Do you have any gin?"

Bug goes on and on, talking about whatever Bug ever talks about, and then, just then, as the meal is coming to a close, the kid looks straight at Vivian, right into her eyes.

"Miss Patsy," he says. "May I ask you to sing a song for my Mama? She's always dreamin' about someday seein' you at the Opry. She's always hummin' along to your record on the jukebox and she just loves your voice. Would you be kind enough to sing a song for her now?"

Bug jerks forward and blabbers: "Now, son, Miss Cline has just finished eating and perhaps, well, yes, in fact, I do believe that we should just leave her be—she just can't—she just can't—you understand, she just can't start singing songs after eating a big, belly-filling meal like this."

But Vivian: She hushes Bug and smiles sweetly and says, "Sure, kiddo, I'd love to. I'm a professional singer, you know."

Bug snaps again: "Her voice may sound different—in fact, yes sir, no doubt, it *will* sound different than on the records because that's the way the records are made and here, well, here without background music,

Miss Patsy, like most singers, well, in fact, like each and every singer will sound different."

Vivian playfully hushes Bug again, sits rigidly and takes a deep breath. Mama and the kid lean forward. They hold hands beneath the table.

Vivian starts snapping her fingers. "I wrote this one myself," she says. Her voice is squeaky, like old bed springs.

"Subway cars, all-night bars
—Oh! How I love New York"

Bug coughs into his napkin and tries to hide his face.

"Downtown lights, all the sights
—Oh! How I love New York"

Mama and the kid: They sit stone-faced.

To Bug's ears the song goes on forever, until Vivian finishes by jumping to her stocking feet, stretching out her sunburned arms and even going so far as to kick a thick, pale leg.

"—Oh! How I love
—Oh! How I love
—Oh! How I love New York!"

Bug: He wants to say something, but for once in his wordy life he can think of nothing to say. Instead, he claps his hands wildly. Neither the kid nor the mother joins in the applause.

The kid watches his mother rise. Bug is still clapping.

"I don't know what in my life I have done to deserve this," Mama says, as Bug finally brings his clapping to a halt. Tears, long and wet tears, come to Mama's eyes. "But that," she says, "was the most beautiful song I have ever heard. Thank you, Miss Patsy."

Mama reaches forward, scoops Vivian's hand into her trembling hand, moves it toward her lips and kisses it gently.

Vivian is all smiles. "Well," she says, "ain't you an angel?"

Bug is by then all grins.

"What'd I tell you?" he is all of a sudden saying. "Miss Patsy Cline," he says. "Miss Patsy Cline herself."

Later, the table cleared, second cups of coffee poured and swallowed, the sun coming closer to the tops of the hills, Bug O'Connor and Vivian

Wynn get ready to leave the roadhouse with full stomachs, a full tank of gas, and a dusty, almost-empty bottle of gin that Mama had "kept under the counter for just-passin'-through salesmen."

Bug and Vivian: They wave to Mama and the kid as they hurry to climb into the convertible and rush to pull onto the road, facing the next rolls of hills. Mama and the kid: They stand at the gas pump, hugging one another, waving good-bye, shouting good luck.

Rolling up the first hill, Vivian squeals, kicks her feet, throws her arms around Bug and kisses his cheek.

"I'm driving, honey," Bug says, tightening his grip on the wheel, keeping his eyes on the narrow road. "What are you celebrating?"

Vivian squeals and kisses him again.

"I must have done something right," she says, "to catch an angel like you."

With that, Bug swallows a deep breath of sunset air and steps deeper on the Buick's accelerator. He's grinning again.

As the convertible dips over the first hill, Mama and the kid stop waving. They silently lower their hands and the smiles melt from their faces.

"I was so nervous," Mama says.

The kid: He starts laughing.

"Patsy Cline," the kid says and spits into the rocky dirt. "Mama, you were just wonderful."

"I do believe I am improvin'," she says, then blushes, then laughs. "Patsy Cline!"

"Patsy Cline," the kid repeats, laughing too and now shaking his head. "'My Mama's always dreamin' about seein' you at the Opry!'"

"Opry!" Mama snorts. She slowly reaches into the big pocket of her house dress and removes Bug's silver cigarette case. "This one's heavy," she says. "Bet it's worth more than all the others put together."

The kid: He grabs the case, tosses it from hand to hand, then turns to face the sullen roadhouse. "We ain't goin' to the Opry, Mama," he says and sighs.

"Chicago!" Mama says. Her big face is as bright as a midnight moon.

The kid smiles. "Now there's a thought," he says. He hangs an arm around his Mama's round shoulders and pulls her close. "Chicago," he says, like he's tasting the word. "Chicago's just the place to make a fresh start."

Things That Matter

Barbara—sometimes I think she's nothing but red lipstick and turtle-necked sweaters—comes charging toward us, smiling, laughing, careful not to spill a drop of merlot from her big wineglass.

"No-no-no," she says. "No talking about movies. Movies are what people talk about when they have nothing else to say."

Bernie says movies are safe. "You can disagree," he explains, "and not really hurt the other person's feelings."

Barbara downs another sip of wine while shaking her head with measured finality. "No," she declares. "This weekend we can only talk about things that matter."

She dashes off into the big kitchen calling for my wife, Claire. That leaves Bernie and me trying to change the subject.

"Books?" I suggest.

"*That* can get too personal," he says.

"The cost of housing?"

He considers, but shakes his head after a thoughtful moment. Thoughtful moments are Bernie's specialty. He's a psychotherapist.

A just-dawned-on-me smile appears from within his short, black beard and makes his balding head wrinkle. "Dogs," he says. "I grew up with a good old German shepherd. Now we've got a dachshund."

"Bernie," I say. "Is this a subject that really matters?"

We laugh together.

This is a weekend intended for laughter. Three couples, longtime friends, gathering on an always-cold, always-snowy January weekend to celebrate Barbara's birthday.

But the rule is we can't ever mention Barbara's birthday. Barbara is big on rules—"Don't ever mention my birthday," "Only talk about things that matter"—but we all love her anyway.

And we all love this house, too, Barbara and Bernie's two-story, four-bedroom getaway on the shores of Lake Michigan in Union Pier. The tall living room windows overlooking the white caps and ice. The wood fireplace snapping with occasional yellow sparks. The woven rugs and polished oak floors.

Claire is in the kitchen with Laura preparing supper, the both of them now trying to convince Barbara they have dinner well under control. Will, Laura's skinny husband, is smoking (and shivering) on the outside deck.

The women's laughter rises in the kitchen—I particularly hear Claire's rather high, somewhat startling guffaw—when I realize I haven't been listening to a single word Bernie has been saying.

"—noise in Calcutta," is where I pick it up. "But that wouldn't discourage us."

I give him what I hope appears to be a confirming nod and grunt, then, try to look surprised at "discovering" the sudden emptiness of my wineglass. "Hey, Bernie," I say, "I need a refill. You?"

He considers, thoughtfully, then, shakes his head.

Claire, Laura and Barbara are friends from way back, high school and college. I always forget which two were friends first and who disliked the other early on, maybe because when the subject comes up they themselves don't seem to agree and they all three talk at once.

Barbara and Bernie have been models, of a sort, for Claire and me. They are a couple who seem made for one another: clearly affectionate, endlessly curious about what the other might have to say, particularly playful with their two small boys, who on this weekend always stay with their wiener dog at Bernie's parents' home in the city.

"You don't think Barbara and Bernie have problems?" Claire has said this to me, more than once, as we've lain awake talking in our beds here and at home. Claire loves conversation, day or night. She produces a public radio talk show. "You always idealize, Ben. They're only human."

"Then why have you started dressing like Barbara?"

"Because—she—I—let's just get some sleep."

Laura and Will have been models of a different sort. The last of the three pairs to marry and the first to display their difficulties in public, Laura and Will always have been the Couple in Trouble, the Couple I Worry About, the Couple I Fear We Might Become.

"Do you hear us?" I have said, more than once, in the midst of a disagreement with Claire. "We're beginning to sound like Laura and Will."

Claire usually frowns when I say this. I think she knows it's true.

Laura co-owns an antiques shop in Winnetka, a hand-me-down from her serious parents that she runs with her youngest sister because she can't stand talking to customers. Will is an audiologist. Their daughter, Bethany, goes to preschool with our son, Adam.

"Are we close to actually eating?" I'm sticking my head inside the swinging kitchen door, wondering if I've just maybe overheard something I shouldn't. The only word I heard clearly was "communion."

The wives are all bent over with the remnant gestures of a good, hard laugh, each of them holding a swaying wineglass by the finger tips.

Claire smiles, snaps to attention and says, "Oops," like she's just been caught. That makes Laura laugh even harder. Barbara steps forward and raises an eyebrow. "Yes," she says. "Benjamin: Yes. Dinner is, indeed, at hand."

I raise an eyebrow, as well. "I'll get Will," I say, starting my retreat from the doorway.

"Oh," Laura says, the thin smile shaping into a sharp grimace on her long face. "Do let my husband smoke."

Smoking is something new for Will. And, what's more, he's smoking cigars.

"I see," I say, and the women laugh with me, though, this time, much of our laughter is uneasy.

"I'm only kidding," Laura adds quickly before I let the swinging door close behind me. "Only kidding. You better retrieve him before the frost-bite really sets in."

Claire and I have spent some time—probably, no doubt, too much time—speculating about the source of Laura and Will's troubles. I have observed, "Well, Laura does have that edge" and Claire has insisted that Will is "the textbook profile to have an affair"—but the evidence of our lives together (at dinners, at movies, at preschool meetings and getaway weekends) has consistently proven Laura's generosity and has never suggested that Will has been anything but faithful.

This past Thanksgiving we thought maybe things would change, soften, between them. That was when Will was diagnosed with tumors.

"How bad is it?" I asked later, over the telephone in mid-December, a hand cupped to my other ear because carolers were singing at our front door.

"Let's put it this way," Will replied. "Nobody's rushing to sell me insurance."

During these past few weeks, however, things haven't mellowed between Laura and Will.

"Sometimes," Bernie explained in a different telephone conversation on a quieter day, "illness only makes people more like themselves."

And so it has with Laura and Will. Sarcasm, a bad habit that launched their romance, now seems to fuel their marriage. "Let's face it," Will told me a few days after our phone conversation. "This has always just been a dress rehearsal for Laura's second marriage."

"Will," I replied, but really didn't know what else to say. Eventually, I changed the subject and asked if he thought taking up smoking at a time like this was a wise idea. He shrugged.

This weekend in Michigan, then, seems much like the others: Laura and Will sniping at one another; Barbara setting rules and Bernie pouring wine; Claire and I swapping behind-their-back looks from time to time. But there is a difference. This weekend, of course, there is new and uncomfortable knowledge beneath all we say and do. There is the fact, unrecognized until now, that this sort of gathering cannot, will not, go on forever. It is something we don't discuss.

Dinner is superb. Stuffed Cornish hens, brown rice, green beans and a dry Bordeaux. While we eat, Barbara commands the conversation, moving us along from subject to subject with laughter and—when a topic like boxing arises, "Oh, please no, let's us talk about anything else"—her authority of having the final word.

Barbara volunteers at the Art Institute as a foreign language interpreter so we spend some time discussing the new exhibit on van Gogh. Then, the performance of our stocks and the diversity of our portfolios. Then, who is and who might be running in our state's gubernatorial race. We speak quickly, words falling upon other words; but certain words are never mentioned.

Will is quiet throughout all of this, his slim shoulders somewhat slumped, his brown eyes forward as he picks at his food. Near the end of the meal, about the time I have placed my silverware on my plate and am taking a final taste of another glass of wine, I look at Claire and catch her yawning and wonder.

Then, Will speaks: "I've got a story," he says. "Maybe you'd all like to hear it?"

The table is suddenly quiet until Laura says, in a voice deliberately too eager, "Oh, yes!"

Will sits back in his chair, but keeps his eyes on the table as if he hasn't heard Laura speak.

"A summer afternoon," he says. "A beach not far from here. A young woman and a young man, wearing black swimsuits and sunglasses. They are stretched out on twin beach chairs. They have been outside sunning for a while now, so they're slightly red and sweaty.

"From time to time, the woman rises and walks the few yards to the lake. She cools her feet on the barest of waves, using one raised hand to shield her face from the glare of the sun as she tries in vain to see the distant city all of the way across the great lake.

"The man smiles as he watches her and, then, as if she feels him smiling, the woman turns her head to see and she smiles, too. 'I could live here forever,' she says.

"Not another soul is on the beach. It's a weekday and, unlike the weekends on this particular stretch of sandy beach, this woman and this man are quite alone. Alone except for each other, that is.

"After another look across the dark blue lake, after taking a lengthy scan of the baby blue sky swept with streaky white clouds, after sighing and stretching and saying it once again—'forever'—the woman returns to the beach chair and sits beside the man.

"The man gives her a moment to get settled, get comfortable. Then, he slowly reaches across the few inches of sand that separates the two of them and he takes her hand in his. She smiles, again, and he smiles, too, because, for now, he still believes in forever."

No one at the table says a word.

Laura brings the white, cloth napkin to her eyes. Barbara looks at Laura. Bernie looks at Will. Claire clutches my hand, her fingernails tight into my skin.

Will looks up. He's smiling. "And Barbara," he says, "I've been meaning to tell you: Happy birthday."

Stations of the Cross

*The Stations of the Cross—sometimes called the Way of Sorrows
or Via Dolorosa—tell the story, in 14 depictions or chapters,
of Christ's final sufferings. Praying at each station is a
popular devotion for many Roman Catholics.*

1. Jesus is Condemned to Death

I'm afraid to tell Zach I love him because I'm certain that will make him
laugh, so instead I place my palm on his bare, warm chest and say, "*Ti amo.*"

We're dancing, in the middle of a pack of slender men, and Zach
squints. He leans closer to shout into my ear above the club's pounding
music. "What?"

"*Ti amo,*" I repeat more loudly. "It's Italian . . . It means, 'You're a
good dancer.'"

Zach likes compliments, so he smiles, nods, kisses me quickly, presses
my hand tighter against his chest, closes his eyes and continues dancing.

2. Jesus is Made to Carry the Cross

I've known Zach for about two weeks. He drives a package delivery
truck. I spend my days working with computers for one of the big banks
downtown. At night, we go out.

3. Jesus Falls for the First Time

Zach and I met at a party hosted by a mutual friend, Simon. Simon is about ten years older and is one of these queens who seems to know everyone. He's also not afraid to wear loads of dangling, gold jewelry.

"*Ecce homo!*" Simon exclaimed, voice and arms high and wide as I stepped inside his glass and chrome condominium for the party.

"Thomas-honey," Simon added more softly as he hugged me tightly. He lowered his voice to whisper conspiratorially. "*Wait* till you see the little gem I've imported for you." Then he ushered me inside to meet a stocky, tanned blonde named Gustav.

4. Jesus Meets His Afflicted Mother

"Gustav," Simon announced. "*This* is Thomas."

Gustav, who was standing with four other guys, turned to face us. The muscles of his arms bulged in short sleeves. All five of those guys boasted bulging biceps in snug short sleeves. Gustav also wore a tiny silver ring in his right earlobe. All five of them sported shiny earrings, as well.

"Gustav works at Argonne National Laboratory," Simon explained. "He's a real Man of Science."

5. Simon of Cyrene Helps Jesus to Carry his Cross

Gustav gave me a slow once-over, a real snobby up-and-down, before sneering and turning his back again, which left us in a cloud of eye-misting cologne. The cologne reminded me of a gag-inducing incense an old boyfriend used to burn.

Simon's eyes opened fiercely, round and wide, but he wasn't really angry. For Simon, matchmaking is a contact sport not unlike rugby: foul play in the scrum is not to be unexpected. I wasn't especially offended, either, perhaps because the introduction had not been anticipated, perhaps because the rejection had come early. Still, I wanted a drink.

6. Veronica Wipes the Face of Jesus

As Simon dashed off to greet yet another guest and I headed toward the Ketel One in the kitchen, I spotted Zach sitting alone on the sofa.

Zach is tall, even when he's sitting. He has green eyes and short, black hair. He smiles often and easily.

Mostly because I had nothing more to lose, I guess, I decided to introduce myself. As Zach stretched to shake hands, he spilled white wine onto his lap. When I said, "Are you trying to baptize yourself?" he smiled. When I offered to help pat him dry, he laughed like he truly hadn't seen that line coming.

It's Zach's laugh that did it for me.

In fact, I am always falling in or out of love with men because of the way they laugh.

7. Jesus Falls the Second Time

By the end of the night, Simon was once again smothering me with hugs and advice: "*Forget* Gustav. He's a quack, anyway. Zach and you are *per*fect together. Plus, the guy's a horse in the hay, Thomas-honey, let me tell you: the stories I've heard? I'm kicking myself for not thinking of the two of you myself. Zach. Is. So. *Sweet*."

I know now Zach and I are perfect together (even if this is a conclusion I have reached after only slightly fewer than fourteen days of our meeting), but I also know Zach isn't exactly what I'd call "sweet."

The night Zach and I left Simon's party, Zach was a little drunk so I offered to drive him home. I unlocked the passenger door for him and by the time I got into the driver's side of my old Volvo, Zach was sitting there, jeans tugged open, legs spread apart.

"Behold," he said, placing a big, warm hand on the back of my head.

Once he finished, he kissed me on my mouth—our first kiss—and laughed. It was an abrupt laugh, full of confidence and faith. "You're going to hate me," Zach said with a broad, bright smile, "but I've got another party. You don't mind dropping me, do you?"

8. Jesus Comforts the Women of Jerusalem

I texted Zach the next afternoon, but didn't hear from him until three evenings later. I wasn't too upset because I have come to learn there are stages in every relationship; some are filled with sacrifice and suffering, others are filled with joy and bliss. The important element is passion and sometimes waiting is the penance we pay for love.

Zach and I agreed to get together and see a movie, a big American film featuring huge, fiery explosions and loud, end-of-world apocalypse rather than the sly, airy Italian comedy I suggested.

Afterward, Zach insisted we head to The Altar, which I thought had been shut down months before but apparently only had been temporarily shuttered for various health violations. A mustached, leather-jacketed, T-shirted doorman was perched at the end of the narrow alley leading to The Altar's entrance. He perked right up when he saw Zach and welcomed him by name.

"Roy," Zach said. "This is my new friend, Thomas."

Roy didn't even bother to look at me. He and Zach moved their faces closer and spoke quietly. A few minutes later, Zach and I headed down the few stairs to enter the dank, dark bar.

It was early still for The Altar and quiet so we went straight to the nearest bartender and ordered beers. I asked Zach what he thought of the movie.

"It was *so* cool," Zach observed, glancing over my shoulder.

"Yes," I said, realizing I was grinning like an overeager acolyte. "It *was* cool."

"I mean," Zach said, as he glanced over my other shoulder and low-ered his voice to express a certain seriousness, "it was *really* cool."

I smiled and nodded, again and again. "It was the coolest movie I've ever seen," I said.

Was I concerned about our lack of profound, meaningful conversa-tion? Confession: Not really. There are, after all, special dispensations one allows during the lustful, initial phases of every relationship.

After a few minutes in silence and several more gulps from beer bot-tles, Zach leaned toward me and spoke in a hushed voice, "You want to go out back, do some poppers?"

I must've made some sort of a face because Zach laughed abruptly and pointed at my face. This was a different kind of laugh, but I found myself quickly saying, "Sure." I was saying "Sure" and I was feeling my face turn red and I so wanted to hear Zach's first laugh again.

As we started walking toward the back of the bar, I wondered whether I should tell Zach I hadn't done poppers since high school. But when he glanced back over his shoulder and actually caught my eye, all I said was, "Lead on."

9. Jesus Falls a Third Time

Two days later Zach called me at work. I was surprised by his call because I had pegged Zach as one of those guys who'd never make the effort.

"There's this great party tonight," he said, speaking quickly. "You want to go?"

"It's Tuesday," I said and immediately felt my face turning red again. Zach was groaning. "—anddd?"

"And sure," I said, picturing Zach's green eyes, thinking of his lips. "Why not? What time?"

"Starts at ten. Pick me up at eleven-thirty."

10. Jesus is Stripped of His Garments

The party was at a bulky, dimly lit house on the city's north side. Zach said he couldn't remember the owner's name. "It's Salva-something, I think."

As we stepped up to the front door, we couldn't help but notice a young, redheaded guy dressed only in a pair of frayed blue jeans, passed out and looking abandoned on the wide porch swing.

"My, my," Zach said, reaching for the door. "The first casualty of the night—already."

"Should we call someone?" I asked. "You think he's okay?"

Zach sighed and smiled at me. "'Not one sparrow can fall to the ground without your Father knowing it,'" he said.

I was stunned. I turned to face Zach. "You know the Bible?"

Zach groaned again, raising his eyebrows. Days later, we'd speak briefly—ever-so briefly—about our Catholic mothers and our on-again, off-again boyhood relationships with the church. I would ask Zach, "Do you think all of these primitive superstitions that people call 'religion' actually do more harm than good?" Zach's gaze would be fixed upon my flat-screened television and he either would not hear my question or he would pretend not to hear my question. I wouldn't bother to ask again.

That night on the porch at the house party, Zach opened the front door, stepped behind me and gently pushed my shoulders. "And a child shall lead them," he said.

Wooden blinds covered the windows. A murky red light filled the place. Boozy music blasted from the living room. Men stripped to their underwear were dancing, necking. Others strolled from room to room, browsing, and not smiling.

I put my mouth near to Zach's ear. "Exactly what kind of party is this?" I said.

"It's a Tuesday party," Zach replied, slipping in front of me as we snaked through the crowd. "Loosen up. This is where I met Simon," he said, then added quickly: "I know, I know. Our buddy Simon doesn't seem the type. But *everyone's* the type. Trust me. Now take off your shirt."

11. Jesus is Nailed to the Cross

An older guy—this was Salva-something, he reminded me of a pot-bellied, wavy-haired church elder from back home—guided us between bodies into the kitchen. He offered beer, margaritas, martinis and—"for old time's sake," as he put it—a dinner plate of ecstasy that was being passed hand-to-hand. Zach and I chose beer.

Salva-something began talking as if he and I had been in the midst of some winding philosophical conversation, but Zach soon interrupted by tapping my shoulder and nodding toward a lanky kid with a shaved head who was leaning against the kitchen doorway. The kid had done his share of working out. His black leather pants were too tight to be buttoned around his slim waist. "Aiden doesn't have a single hair on his entire body," Zach explained. "So, what do you think?"

I put my mouth to Zach's ear again. "I think Aiden looks like he maybe kills rabbits," I said and turned and tried to refocus on my sort-of conversation with Salva-something.

The next time I noticed, Zach was across the kitchen, whispering into the bald kid's ear. Aiden zeroed in on me and smiled crookedly beneath slightly crossing eyes. Zach waved me over.

"Thomas," Zach said, "meet my old friend, Aiden."

The bald kid grunted.

"Well," Zach said. "Now that the introductions are out of the way, what do you say we three head upstairs?"

There are times when we do things we wouldn't usually do, let alone ever do—times when we are driven by a blind faith that overpowers that which some call Better Judgment. Zach wrapped his left arm around Aiden's wispy waist and his right arm around mine. "Trust me," Zach whispered into my ear.

12. Jesus Dies on the Cross

Zach, Aiden and I headed upstairs to a small, unoccupied bedroom. The room had white painted walls, an unmade bed, no pillows, a wooden chair and a tall, black floor lamp that was lit with a single red light bulb. Aiden unlaced his boots and began to peel off his pants. Zach smiled at me again, taking the beer bottle from my hands. "Here," he said, clutching my shoulders and turning me toward him. "You get to be the Man in the Middle."

We were all still standing. Zach steered my shoulders until I felt Aiden poking against me from behind. I did not flinch. But I did say: "Hey. Do you mind if we at least close the door?"

Zach frowned and looked at Aiden over my shoulder. "Thomas is a small town boy," he sighed, pretending to pout. "He's shy and not yet accustomed to our big city ways."

Later, with the three of us naked, exhausted and sprawled across the bed like some unholy Trinity, Aiden leaned over me to kiss Zach on the cheek. Aiden smelled like an old pair of winter gloves. I heard him tell Zach, "You know I love you . . ."

And that's when Zach laughed.

Zach tried not to laugh but he apparently couldn't keep himself from laughing.

The skin tightened where Aiden's eyebrows should've been and the guy's narrow eyes suddenly looked slippery with tears.

"Don't laugh," Aiden moaned. Then, softer: "Please don't laugh."

"I'm—sorry," Zach stammered. But he was still laughing heartily. "It's just that your idea of love is very different than my idea of love."

"Up yours," Aiden snapped and began squirming out from beneath all of our limbs to bolt out of bed.

"Wait," Zach shouted, but we all knew it was too late. "I'm sorry," Zach said, sitting up, almost sounding sincere. "Forgive me! Look— we're having fun—don't ruin it—there's no need to get all—"

Aiden snatched his pants and boots from the floor and glared back at us before slamming the door on his way out.

I looked at Zach, who seemed genuinely sorry. Or maybe he was just sleepy. He grunted and dropped backward onto the bed mattress beside me. "Wow," he sighed. "Another casualty."

13. Jesus is Taken Down from the Cross

Zach now tells me he wants to take a break from dancing, so we walk through the crowd to the bar.

"The music is *so* cool tonight," Zach shouts above the throbbing noise.

"Yes" I reply, pretending not to know and not to care that this is as penetrating as any of my conversations with Zach will ever go. The suffering of that particular observation is still to come. "It's really cool," I say, realizing I cannot for the life of me take my eyes off of him.

"Good-looking crowd, too."

"Yes," I say. "Indeed."

14. Jesus is Laid in the Tomb

After a while, Zach and I are dancing again. The music pounds, the lights flash.

Zach smiles and I find myself thinking of fallen sparrows and broken hearts. I'm remembering first kisses and long nights at The Altar and poor-though-surely-not-innocent Aiden. I place my open palm upon Zach's chest once more.

"Your hand is warm," he says.

Zach smiles, presses closer and I catch myself wanting to tell him. It's only been two weeks, I know, but, just for a moment, I picture introducing Zach as "my boyfriend," sitting across from him and pouring tall glasses of pinot grigio at dinner parties *we're* hosting, cuddling with Zach as we sit in bed watching travel videos about Tuscany. I feel myself about to speak when I realize that in all of my fantasies, there's something I no longer imagine.

I no longer imagine Zach laughing.

The Second Time

After I moved to Chicago the second time I fell in with a crowd of young artists even though I felt old enough to be everyone's father. They were playwrights and poets, painters and actors. They gathered at the shaded, sidewalk tables of a small, Lakeview coffeehouse named Beans. Back when I lived in Chicago the first time—years ago, I had moved from Louisiana to marry a school nurse named Sheanna and to pursue sweet dreams of someday becoming a big-time jazz piano player—there were no such coffee shops in town.

"Mister, we need your opinion."

That was my invitation into the clique. On this particular morning— a bright, breezy June Sunday—Peter, Ami, James, Leslie and Seth were sitting outside, congregated around a tiny, round table. They were sipping iced mochas from plastic cups and eating fresh blueberry muffins on paper napkins. A sable-and-tan-colored dog was curled at their feet.

"Ami doesn't trust a thing we tell her," Peter added quickly as the others laughed. Peter is a skinny, white kid who's almost always grinning; in fact, they're all thin and rather smiley—except for Seth, who, like me, carries his stocky self just a bit too seriously.

"Maybe she'll listen to you," Peter continued. He has large, blue eyes and was wearing narrow, black-rimmed eyeglasses, a white T-shirt and khakis. I was sitting alone at the next table.

Ami—a strawberry blonde with pale, almost shiny skin—was turning tomato red.

The others laughed again as Peter tilted backward on his wobbly chair, leaned an elbow onto my table and said: "Just give us the poem, Ami. This guy will have an objective opinion."

The cajoling continued for another few uneasy moments, during which I caught Leslie and Seth sneaking sideways looks at me. Leslie has round, dark eyes and a boxy jaw. She wears her curly, black hair in a way that makes her look frumpy. She later admitted being wary about pulling me into their conversation, but making nice with all kinds of strangers was exactly the sort of thing Peter was always doing. Seth was giving me the once-over, too, as he pretended to pet his sleeping collie, which, I later learned, also is named Seth.

As the group's chatter grew more raucous, I began to feel awful for Ami. The situation reminded me of how my old man back in New Orleans used to wake me in the middle of the night to hammer out tunes on the dusty, off-key upright in our dimly lit living room as he banged around the kitchen, mixing large rum-and-Cokes for one or another of his flashy, loud, late-night girlfriends. Such sudden, drunken coaxing made my talent feel small.

"I really don't know much about poetry," I offered, hoping that might calm the crowd and get Ami off the hook.

"But that's exactly what she wants," James said loudly. James is tall and droopy-eyed. He has a black goatee and says everything abruptly. "Someone who doesn't know anything to tell her how wonderful her poetry is."

That silenced everyone until Peter planted his chair firmly on the ground, yanked himself closer to their table and said to Ami, "Well?" Then, we all looked at Ami to see how she'd respond.

She made a face.

I've now come to recognize the look: the tip of her tongue between thin, parted lips; the slight lift of her chin—it signals a decision has been reached.

"Don't do anything you don't want—" Leslie began, but Ami rose, turned toward me, stared directly into my eyes and spoke:

> *"And why did you*
> *come back to me?*
> *To whisper my name—*
> *hear me sigh*
> *To hold my hand—*
> *make me cry*
> *To chase my heart—*
> *please don't lie*
> *To kiss my soul—*
> *and say good-bye?"*

Everyone was silent. Ami continued to look at me.

"That's it," she said. "That's all."

I sensed everyone else was looking at me, as well.

"That's the greatest poem I've ever heard," I announced and the table erupted with laughter. Ami's face grew an even deeper shade of red. "I'm serious," I protested as she sat and crossed her arms. "I'm really serious."

Peter stood, slapped my back, called me, "My man," and offered to buy me a coffee. From then on I was their friend. But no one, I think— least of all, Ami—understood how much I had meant what I had said.

My new friends worked "real" jobs to support their art. Peter the playwright wrote snappy newspaper advertisements. James scolded Peter again and again for limiting his vision and squandering his gifts. Such work, James insisted, would only ensure that Peter might one day pen the "Great American Blurb."

But James shouldn't have been so critical. He was a jumpy abstract painter who was always scrambling from carpentry job to carpentry job with his two older brothers. "You cannot believe how expensive it is to paint," he often bemoaned.

Leslie considered herself a playwright, as well. She was married to an insurance adjuster and taught nighttime college classes of English-as-a-second-language. She'd bow her heavy head and scribble dramatic scenes while her mostly Eastern European students stammered in small groups or while her husband slept soundly beside her in bed.

Seth was an actor who waited tables. I never went to his restaurant. Ami the poet also waited tables. I visited her restaurant frequently.

The place was called The Trinity Knot. It was situated just down the shop-lined block from Beans, on Southport Avenue across from the old Movie Box Theatre. Trinity's was a not-too-big, not-too-busy pub that didn't get loud until later and served overpriced sandwiches, which I couldn't really afford. The tables were square and close together. The chairs were upholstered in faded plaid.

"Written me any new poems lately?" I had fallen into the habit of asking this question when Ami would approach my table. She'd smile widely, look down, brush a few strands of stray hair behind her right ear and say, "Not lately. How are you, B.J.?"

"Me?" I'd say. "I'm doing a hundred, shifting down to ninety."

"You back to playing any music yet?"

"Not yet. Been a long time. Too long, probably."

"Beer—no glass?"

"You got it."

From the start, I had an overwhelming crush on Ami. She was young and genuine and hopeful—and nothing at all like me. When Sheanna had called off our wedding engagement years ago, one of the last things she had said to me was: "We're too much alike, B.J. We'd never stand a chance together."

"Maybe I could play something for you sometime," I told Ami one of the first evenings I stopped at Trinity after work.

"That'd be wonderful," she said, smiling. "Just let me know when and where you happen to find a piano."

I had been back in Chicago for about two months. I was working the morning shift at a cardboard box factory within walking distance from Beans and The Trinity Knot, along Ravenswood Avenue. The work was mindless; the pay, meager. I was staying with a friend around the corner, renting a cramped backstairs bedroom until I could put aside a few more dollars.

I had abandoned piano playing shortly after Sheanna had given up on me, though the tunes were still constantly rolling through my head, keeping me awake most nights.

"If you still hear it, you haven't lost it," Ami reassured me one evening. But, honestly, I wasn't sure if I even wanted to play piano again and, besides, I had no idea where I would find one to try.

When I'd meet the crowd at Beans, I'd occasionally be introduced to other young artists and the gang would start talking about art—dissecting some new novel I hadn't heard of, debating the weaknesses of this or that obscure play or foreign film. Peter led most conversations and James was in charge of disagreeing. Leslie showed up less and less frequently. Seth had taken up smoking hand-rolled cigarettes—for an upcoming stage role, he explained. Ami and I mostly just listened. It had been some time since I had been around people with dreams and ambitions and heartfelt opinions.

As much as I appreciated those times—they woke me up after perforating and stacking boxes all day—I much more enjoyed going to The Trinity Knot. There, without the crowd, Ami and I had an opportunity to get to know one another, though, at first, we mostly spoke about the others.

James had just finished a new painting, but was already complaining about it, proclaiming his work a failure. I gathered that James was always full of sharp complaints and blustery judgments. Ami agreed.

"But you've got to cut him some major slack," she cautioned, her head slowly nodding. "James would be there for you if you ever really needed a hand."

She was less enthusiastic about Leslie.

"She's nice and all, don't get me wrong," Ami confided on a different day, "but I think she thinks I need a big sister. And I think she wants a baby more than she ever wants to finish her play."

We could agree on Seth. "He's a bit into himself," I observed. "Totally," Ami grinned. "The best thing about Seth is Seth the Dog."

Whenever we got around to talking about Peter, though, Ami's face would brighten and her eyes would grow dreamy and I'd find myself fumbling to change the subject. A few times I suggested she recite a poem, but once she recited a "brokenhearted" poem she had written while thinking of Peter, so I tried changing the subject yet again.

"Hey," I said, "we should go to a mall. I could play for you using one of those store pianos."

As the weeks passed, I began visiting The Trinity Knot almost every evening Ami worked. I never asked her for a date, probably because the more I got to know her, the more charmed I became and the more foolish I felt. I was too old for her, I told myself. Too uninformed about poetry. Too scared.

"I've been meaning to ask you something," Ami said one slow night. The place was nearly empty and she was standing beside my table at the window. Outside, Southport Avenue was being splattered with an August rain. "Why'd you ever come back to Chicago?"

"To see an old friend." My answer wasn't entirely untrue, but the complete reason was more complicated: I had returned to attend Sheanna's funeral.

About a year after she had ended our engagement and I left town, Sheanna met and married a good man named Terrence. They had two kids, boys. Sheanna continued working as a school nurse and even stayed in touch with me, from time to time, through my father down in New Orleans. In fact, it had been through my father that I had met Sheanna in the first place. Sheanna's Auntie had been one of my father's best girlfriends and more frequent late-night guests.

When I heard from Terrence through my father that Sheanna had passed, I scraped together what little money I could, purchased a train ticket and returned to Chicago. At the funeral, I learned that Sheanna had been sick for some time. I was also surprised when Terrence introduced me to their two little ones, saying, "This is the Uncle B.J. that Mommy was always telling you about." The boys smiled shyly and their big eyes grew even bigger.

After the service, Terrence invited me to stay in their backstairs bedroom and even offered to hire me for a job at the box factory he managed.

But this was more about me than I had ever explained to anyone, so I simply told my poet friend Ami: "Her name was Sheanna. We had been real close at one time, but it didn't work out and now she's gone."

Ami said, "Oh, I'm sorry," and looked down, once again brushing a few strands of hair behind her ear. She sighed.

"How about you?" I asked. I knew Ami had been born and raised in a small farm town in southern Illinois.

Ami looked outside at the rain hitting the parked cars and otherwise empty pavement. "I grew up wondering about big cities," she explained, "and, well, sometimes you've just got to roll them dice."

I laughed hard whenever Ami spoke fake-tough like that, but I wasn't laughing a few nights later when she suddenly sat in the vacant chair across my table at Trinity.

"B.J.," she said, "I know we haven't known each other for too long, but there's something I need to ask you."

She seemed nervous. Her narrow shoulders were slumped forward. I sipped my bottle of beer. Ami glanced at two tables of other customers, then leaned closer.

"Do you think Peter loves me?" Her blue eyes looked into mine.

"Peter?" I said and she nodded.

The tip of her tongue appeared between her lips. Her chin lifted slightly. "Because the truth is, I'm crazy about him." Her face brightened. "He's so beautiful and he has a way of making me believe in my poetry."

I listened and exhaled slowly. There was much to say to all of that, but what I said was: "The only thing I know for sure is he'd be crazy not to love you."

Ami thought about that and sat back in the chair. She quickly exchanged looks with her manager, a heavy-set Irishman wiping up the bar who frowned upon seeing her seated at my table. Then she looked at me again. She smiled. "You love me, too, don't you, B.J.?"

"Me?" I said, nearly choking on my beer. "You?"

She nodded, smiled widely, bit her lower lip. "I knew it," she said. "It's not exactly hard to tell." She stood and straightened her shoulders. "Let me ask you this: Why do you love me?"

I raised my eyebrows. There was plenty to say to that, as well.

Ami spoke softly. "Is it because I remind you of her? Do I remind you of Sheanna?"

It was my turn to smile. I reached across the table and held Ami's small, soft hand.

"Only on the inside," I said.

The following weekend, I invited Ami to join me on a short, morning walk around our neighborhood of two-flats, six-flats and brick homes.

The sun was shining and we didn't speak much as we strolled. More than once, as we passed occasional young women and men pushing baby strollers or walking dogs, Ami looked up at me to ask, "Are you okay, B.J.?"

"I'm fine," I'd say and keep walking.

"Did I make you mad the other day?"

"No," I'd say and keep walking.

I was thinking about dreams and love, possibility and hope. I was hearing the echo of a phrase contained in Ami's brokenhearted poem about Peter: "We never stop learning about love."

Finally, we came to a two-story white house that was undergoing some extensive renovations. Sheets of dark blue plastic covered the upstairs windows. The small front yard was strewn with sawhorses, two-by-fours and a bucket.

Ami glanced at the house, then back to me. "I don't get it," she said. "What are we doing here?"

I held out my hand. She smiled and placed her warm hand in mine, saying, "B.J.?"

I led her up the front porch steps, opened the unlocked door and stepped inside. When she hesitated, I said, "It's okay. We've got our friend, James the painter-carpenter, to thank."

Ami laughed, shaking her head. "Should I be trusting you?"

"Baby," I said, "sometimes you've just got to roll them dice."

She laughed again and stepped inside. I closed the door.

We heard work boots scuffling across the wooden floors upstairs: James and his two brothers.

Ami raised her eyebrows. "B.J., why are we here?"

Her eyes were bright and wide. This would've been the perfect moment to kiss her, but I knew she didn't want that and instead I only smiled and stepped aside to let her look passed me, around the oak staircase and into the living room. Big white sheets covered a sofa, two armchairs and a baby grand piano in the corner.

I walked to the piano, swept aside the sheet, sat on the black bench and began to play. I had almost forgotten the cool, light feel of the piano keys and, after a moment, I had to stop to find my place. But then I picked up again and, still smiling as Ami smiled at me, played a quiet song I had long ago written for Sheanna.

The Jonquils

Kenneth Collins is doing what Kenneth Collins always does when Kenneth Collins is anxious: repeating a silent prayer, the "Hail Mary," again and again until the boredom of repetition subdues his nerves. Of course, boredom is not the point of prayer, but boredom is what Kenneth Collins desires. Dull, plain, safe boredom.

As he recites the prayer, Kenneth Collins watches his ex-wife take a seat at the dining room table as his new wife ushers one of his dead son's friends to the smaller table that showcases all of the memorial photographs.

When Kenneth Collins sees Vince—his dead son's lover, his dead son's boyfriend, his dead son's "partner," that is— Kenneth Collins finds himself wanting to pray again. "Hail Mary, full of grace," he says to himself. "The Lord is with thee."

ROY GETS A GLIMPSE OF HIMSELF

Words, words, nothing but fucking words and no words at all about fucking. And that was the great thing about Jordan, though you wouldn't know it by anything that was said at the memorial this afternoon. Jordan was a great lay, one of the all-time best lays, one of those dark-haired, make-you-sweat, break-your-back boys who aren't supposed to exist in real life.

But Jordan did exist in real life.

And I loved him.

And I miss him.

To tell the truth, there hasn't been one fucking morning or one fucking night this whole past year when I haven't thought about Jordan. And that surprises me. That surprises me because I knew I loved Jordan—but I didn't know I loved him this much.

GRETCHEN CELEBRATES A SUCCESS

Still upset about the artichoke dip. Turned out much too runny. But, the rest of the table—the spinach dip and the garbanzo spread, the cucumber fingers and the carrot sticks, the cauliflower buds and the green pepper rings, the cheeses, the mushroom pâté, the red onion potato salad and so on—why, it was all just splendid. And the house looked wonderful, too, for once. Since Ken finally listened to me and fired Gabriella and hired Gracie, this old place has never looked better. The floors. The oak staircase. And, yes, the flowers were perfect, too. Jonquils! Muted yellow in crystal vases. Not at all morose and certainly not overly chipper. Just right—just perfect, surrounded by all of the framed photographs of Jordie.

BONNIE FINDS MORE TIME FOR DISAPPOINTMENT

Mom held up so much better than I ever expected and she looked great now that she's losing all that weight. When she gets way down, Dad's going to be sorry and not just sorry about dumping Mom for Gretchen and leaving us, but sorry about everything—*every*thing.

I can't believe he didn't even cry—all afternoon and not a single tear. The house is shoulder-to-shoulder with people blubbering away—Mom, me, family friends, Vince, Jordie's other friends—all of us, weeping, and Dad just stands there, hands in his pockets, eyes to the floor. Like he's waiting for a bus. Some big, white bus to pick him up and drive him away, take him away from all of us for good and take him away from himself and Jordie and any other ghosts who haunt him.

And what about when it was his turn to talk?

"My name is Kenneth Collins and I want to start by thanking you all for coming"—like he was opening one of his sales meetings. "There's somebody named Jordan Collins who means something very important to each of us"—like Jordie was this month's top seller.

Dad even had his wide, sales smile, too, and he held his head back, chin up, in that way he always does when he's really only talking about himself. Everyone else had something sweet to remember about Jordie, the time he did this, the time he said that. But all Dad could muster was his usual crap, his typical Dad B.S., his—

Is that the baby crying?

Vince is trying not to laugh. He recalls a variety of feelings from these past few months—the hollowness, the sorrow, the loneliness, the choking anger, the relief, the guilt over feeling relieved, the numbing fear—and suddenly, now, he feels like guffawing.

Of course, laughing is not a sin.

Vince is standing in the big kitchen, asking Bonnie and Gracie if they need help. They say no, explaining how they prepared each and every dish, how they changed their minds, how Gretchen had the final say.

But all Vince is thinking about is Jordie: How Jordie must be looking down from Heaven and loving this party because Jordie, once again, is the very center of attention.

"Vince?" Bonnie says. "Why are you smiling?"

ROY SINGS A SONG

I tell the cab driver to hop on Lake Shore Drive, to take the long way home, and I ask myself this question: How come Jordan and I never really got together? "Dated," I mean. "Lived together." As boyfriends.

We'd known each other for almost seven years, since I moved up from Maple Park. We had pretty much the same life, early on: a series of those fast, hard, three- or four-month relationships; but always with somebody else, never with each other. We'd always been friends and, sometimes, hell, a lot of times, we'd slept together. But we never spent even two nights in a row together. It was always wake up, get out of bed quick, tell each other how great the sex was (the truth, but let's not even glance at one another) and then make some mostly-serious joke about never messing around again because it would someday, certainly, without doubt, ruin our friendship (a lie, but let's exchange meaningful looks and knowing nods).

Christ. I suppose—no, in fact, I know for a fact—that Jordan was far better off with Vincent than he ever would've been with me. Vincent stuck it out through the end with Jordan—hell, Vincent is still sticking it out with Jordan—and, let's face it, that's more than I can say for myself.

I don't think I would've stuck it out. I don't have the sort of guts you need for the Stand-By-His-Side routine. *This*, friendship, is tough enough.

But, who knows? Who the fuck ever knows?

To think of all the shit Vincent had to put up with—and I don't just mean all the sick shit, all the hospital shit, all the dying shit: I mean the family shit, the Collins Shit. None of them ever really warmed to Vincent, made him feel welcomed. Vince used to say it probably had more to do with Mr. and Mrs. Collins divorcing than with him and Jordan getting together, but I doubt it. And Bonnie was no help, with her blockheaded banker husband and the way they kept the twins and the baby away from Jordan after Vincent moved in—and particularly after Jordan got sick.

Fuck that. Just look at this afternoon: The kids? Nowhere in sight. Probably home with Papa Beancounter. And Mr. Collins? He stood in one corner, while Vince lingered in another, both of them looking like they were worried about getting arrested for loitering.

Vincent has always done his best to smooth over the family distance— "They're all very nice people, really . . . Every family has its quirks"—but when I brought my little plate over to him this afternoon, he whispered, "Do you see them? Do you see the way they all stare at me like I'm the other shoe waiting to drop?"

This was still early, so I tried smiling instead of frowning. "'We— Are—Fam-i-ly,'" I pretended to sing and that at least got Vincent to laugh. He laughed so hard, some red came to his cheeks.

"Now," he said, "you sound like Jordie."

GRETCHEN CONSIDERS AN ACT OF GENEROSITY
Have to tell Ken—if he *ever* gets himself out of that bathroom—that I'm more than happy with Gracie's work. Really couldn't have pulled off today without her. Maybe we can slip her a little extra something.

The day just went so well.

. . . All things considered.

BONNIE COULD HAVE TOLD YOU
Vince looked good. Healthy. I wonder how he's doing, how he's feeling, how he's holding up.

He certainly seemed fine and he had so many funny, funny stories about Jordie. He's always had so many funny stories about Jordie: The time they went to that party on that yacht and Jordan—wearing his black tuxedo, juggling three bottles of prosecco—slipped off the gangplank and went ass over teacups into Belmont Harbor . . . The time Jordie insisted that they give a lift to that hitchhiking nun near Montreal . . . The time Jordan invented his Three Rules for a Happy Life: "One: Always tip the bartender. Two: Never say no to a man named Marcello. And three: Live—and let live already."

Everyone laughed when Vince recalled the rules, but I looked around.

Dad was fake laughing and Gretchen's eyebrows were arched high enough to spell, "My, My!"

Kenneth Collins is fumbling with his eyeglasses, taking them off, putting them on. Kenneth Collins walks over to Vince and opens his mouth to speak, but Gretchen taps his shoulder.

Of course, Gretchen doesn't know any better.

"Dear," she says to Kenneth Collins. "The bean salad. Be a lamb."

ROY TURNS RED

I don't know why today pissed me off. I've been to other memorials—countless other memorials, for Christ's sake—and I've never been bothered like this before. Maybe, today, the memories just echoed with too much hypocrisy. According to Vincent, there had been so little remembering for so long. I don't know. Maybe I just shouldn't have been there. Maybe I'm just tired of people still getting sick and people still dying. Maybe I'm just tired of always having to remember. Maybe—maybe maybe maybe, always a thousand fucking maybes.

At the very least, I shouldn't have spent so much time talking to Vincent. He reminds me too much of Jordan. The way they both stand, relaxed, all the weight on one foot. The way they both laser beam their blue eyes right into yours when they're talking. At the very least, one minute less with Vincent and I wouldn't have asked that stupid fucking question: "Do you miss the sex?"

The way Vincent looked at me, I couldn't blame him.

"I'm sorry," I started to mumble. "I didn't mean to—"

But by then Vincent was smiling again, touching my elbow, telling me not to apologize.

"Sex with Jordan was the best sex I ever had," he explained, broadening his smile.

Right then, Jordan's real Mom walked passed and the three of us shared polite, wordless nods. She's a big woman and she's always been kind of pleasantly batty, but she was his mother for Christ's sake and I could feel myself turning red—something, you can bet your ass, which hasn't happened in a long fucking time.

Then Vincent leaned closer toward me, lowered his voice. "But you know what Jordan liked doing the most?"

I couldn't help it. My mind flipped back to three years and before, shuffling through a catalog of blowjobs, handjobs, and late nights filled with squeezed muscles, jabbing boners and wet tongues.

"What?" I asked.

Tears slipped into Vincent's eyes. "Kissing," he said. "Jordan loved kissing the most."

I couldn't help thinking how little Jordan and I had ever actually pressed our lips together.

"Kissing?" I said.

"Yeah," Vincent said. He nodded, still smiling, still leaning close. "Jordan used to say that everything else was just foreplay to an orgasm—and an orgasm was something you could always give yourself. But a kiss, he said, a kiss means you need someone else there with you. Someone to hold."

GRETCHEN GETS MIFFED

Can't believe he's asleep already.

"G'night," he says and climbs under the covers, turns his back to me.

Yes, the party was his idea. *Yes*, I, at first, did object. But once I was on board, Ken turned it all over to me—today was my baby!—and, may I say, today was a triumph.

But now he gives me this: his back and his silence. No "thank-you." No "the-place-looked-beautiful-today-darling." No "you-were-simply-fantastic-this-afternoon."

Just a "G'night"—and this: his back.

BONNIE WEEPS

The thing that irks me the most about Gretchen is the way she refers to Jordie as Jordie. Like she ever really knew him. Like she was his "Mother," like they were close. She has no right calling Jordie Jordie.

The other thing that really irks me is the way she managed to make herself busy just when Mom arrived. "Bonnie," she had said, in that way of hers, that way that just makes my shoulders pinch together. "Be a dear and see who's at the door. Gracie and I *must* finish chopping our carrots!"

She smiled then, like she and Gracie were best and dearest friends, like she's not constantly picking on that poor old woman, telling her the "right" way to do this, do that.

I should've said something.

Why didn't I say something?

Gretchen knew very well who was at the damn door. She had seen Mom's car pull up the drive just as I had.

And she knew very well who was ringing the bell when Vince arrived, too. She wasted no time swooping to the door to greet him—"Vince, sweet, poor Vince! Come inside, quick, before you catch cold!"

She made sure to say it loudly enough so we all could hear, even back in the kitchen.

And then, before she's even got the door closed, she's badgering him—"Did you remember to bring a picture? Can you believe how cold it's gotten again? Did you forget your photograph of Jordie for the table? I thought winter was over."

Vince tugged a photograph out of his gray overcoat pocket—a large, gold-framed shot of Jordie grinning, looking back over his right shoulder, standing barefoot in jeans on a sunny southwest Michigan beach.

"It's a little out of focus," Vince said.

"Nonsense," Gretchen shrieked.

"But it was Jordie's favorite picture of himself," Vince said.

"It's perfect!" Gretchen said, flashing her witch's smile, getting her claws around the frame and scampering off to the narrow table beneath the picture window with all of the flowers. "Just perfect!"

I was out of the kitchen by then, so I walked around and took Vince's coat to hang up.

"Hi, Bonnie," he said, stooping to give me a hug. I had forgotten how tall Vince is. We pressed our cheeks together and then he went over to hug that spooky Roy and all those other guys.

For a minute, I stood there holding onto Vince's coat, and when I turned to hang it up, it hit me: This is the coat of my dead brother's lover, I thought. This is the coat of another dying young man. And then I started to cry. Silent tears. Private tears. The first of my many tears today. And I thank God the kids weren't there to catch me crying. God knows I saw my own mother crying way too often, way too much.

> *Vince is standing at the door, putting on his coat, calling thanks to Gracie, telling Bonnie how good it was to see her again, how he really must see the twins and the new baby sometime soon.*
> *Bonnie nods.*
> *"Thank you for everything," Vince tells Jordan's mom, and she smiles, hugging him without saying a word. "And thanks for all of your hard work," Vince tells Gretchen.*
> *"Oh, it was nothing," Gretchen says loudly, "nothing— nothing at all."*
> *Kenneth Collins hands Vince a pair of gray gloves that had slipped from Vince's coat pocket. The two men pause for a moment, their hands almost touching.*
> *"You know," Kenneth Collins says, his voice barely a whisper, his eyes on the gloves. "I guess I never imagined that Jordan would die before me."*
> *Vince bites his lower lip and finds himself looking at the gloves, as well. "I know," he says, taking the gloves into his*

hands, allowing his eyes to lift and meet Kenneth Collins' for just a moment. Of course, both men want to say so much, but both men feel the lateness of the day.
   "I know," Vince says again.
   "Yes," Kenneth Collins says.
   "I know."

ROY MAKES A DECISION

When my time comes, I'm going to insist on no memorials. I'm going to leave orders: burn my body, flush the ashes down the toilet, and get on with your fucking little lives.

No Collins Shit for me, with people whispering, with everyone talking about the "dearly departed" but only really thinking about themselves, with the drapes half-drawn as if the fucking house was still half-hiding some big secret, with everyone but Vincent afraid to even speak aloud the scarlet letters.

No sir. No memorial. Not for me.

No way. No more chances to fuck-up a good-bye. No.

I'll die and that'll be it.

I'll die—and it'll all just be over.

Over and out.

GRETCHEN HOLDS HER GROUND

Bones to him, is what I say. Bones to him—and his lack of gratitude.

BONNIE TELLS A STORY ABOUT HER MOTHER

Earlier, after we had listened to all of the speeches and nibbled all of the desserts, Gretchen herded us around the photo table and we eventually began swapping more stories about Jordan. But a few minutes into it, Gretchen starts fondling this one picture of Jordie pretending to pout. She sighs, dramatically, and then, trying to be witty, I guess, she says, "He was *such* a good looking young man! Speaking as a woman, it's too bad he was gay!"

I could feel my stomach knot and I could see Vince come *this* close to a scream. Dad didn't say a word, of course. And the rest of us stayed quiet, too.

But then we heard Mom say, "Narcissus."

We all turned to look at her.

She was sitting apart from all of us, in a straight-back dining room chair near the kitchen door. She was wearing her new, dark purple dress. She was balancing a teacup and saucer on her lap. She was smiling brightly.

"Why I mean the flowers, of course," she said. "The jonquils. Their family name." Still smiling, she looked directly at us, taking her time with each and every one of us. I remembered a late night from child-hood in this very house, hours of bickering in the deepening darkness that finally ended when Dad shouted that Mom's "big-eyed smile" was driving him nuts.

Mom was smiling that smile now. She nodded toward the flowers. "They're beautiful, no?"

The Wedding

Everyone applauds as the Groom kisses the Groom. The guests rise from their white, wooden chairs that are sprawled beneath two wide, white canopies flapping in the sunny breeze. They continue clapping as the Grooms, now holding hands, grin and turn to face their guests.

The priest stands behind the couple, her arms held apart as if to embrace the two men and lift them and say—*Behold*. The priest is grinning, too. Behind her is a wide garden of big rocks and tall prairie grass that marks the end of the long yard and the top of the steep sand dunes, which lead to Lake Michigan.

It is a cool afternoon in late spring.

The Grooms kiss again and step forward to hug their families in the front row of guests. Richard's mother and father adore Brendan. Brendan's mother loves Richard like a second son. Brendan's father passed away a few years earlier.

—*I almost cried, but I held it together,* Brendan says to his family. He's smiling broadly.

—*Well, I did cry,* says Richard's father, the retired Colonel. He grins, too, and squeezes Brendan's shoulder.

—*Really?* Brendan raises his eyebrows. The Colonel, a man so seemingly different from his own father, always has intimidated him.

—*Yes,* the Colonel says, shaking his head, *of course. What you don't know about men.*

Everyone laughs.

A pianist, bassist and drummer are situated behind the twelve rows of chairs near the stone patio that wraps around the rear of Richard's parents' house. The trio begins playing a brisk version of, "The Man I Love."

In the crowd, one of Richard's cousins begins snapping his fingers. Brendan's half-sister, Bridget, holds onto her floppy hat and widens her eyes and giggles with her young daughter.

Everyone is happy.

The bearded photographer slips carefully through the crowd, snapping pictures of jovial men wearing business suits, cheerful women wearing bright dresses and restless children wearing "good" shoes.

The six bartenders begin mixing and serving drinks. An army of caterers quickly lifts lids from warming dishes, which fill five buffet tables on the patio.

Brendan is speaking with a small cluster of guys when he hears the jazz trio begin, "Our Love is Here to Stay." He turns quickly to look for Richard among the guests. He almost shouts his husband's name because he does not want to miss their first dance.

Then: From above the crowd or through the crowd or as if it were emanating from within this crowd of friends and family, Brendan hears an echo of a familiar voice—*Be still*—a memory, his father, speaking at a time when Brendan and Bridget were quite young. *Be still.*

And Brendan calms and turns and sees Richard stepping forward from the crowd.

The two men gaze into one another's eyes, embrace, and begin dancing.

What You Don't Know About Men is Michael Burke's first book. He also is the author of the plays *Wama-Wama Zing Bing* and *Let's Spend Money.* He lives in Chicago, and his blog—www.ChicagoWriter.blogspot.com—features book reviews, social commentary and political opinion.